AROUND TOWN
The Elliotts strike again!

Manhattan's wealthiest family is once again hitting the tabloids, thanks this time to playboy Cullen Elliott. While the sexy sales director of *SNAP* magazine has been seen escorting some of the city's most beautiful women, Cullen has been hiding a deep, dark secret—a mistress hidden away in the playground known as Sin City.

According to reliable sources, Cullen's secret lover is Misty Vale, a long-legged, green-eyed ex-showgirl straight from the Vegas strip.

And he's brought her to Manhattan. To introduce her to his parents—editor Daniel and attorney Amanda Elliott—in anticipation of his pending nuptials, perhaps? New York society holds its breath to hear the respectable family's reaction.

The rumor mill is abuzz over on Park Avenue where the Elliott publishing empire holds court. Something—or someone—major had to have pushed the confirmed bachelor to propose. Could it be the mistress is carrying an Elliott heir?

We'll be following the story....

Dear Reader,

Thanks for choosing Silhouette Desire this month. We have a delectable selection of reads for you to enjoy, beginning with our newest installment of THE ELLIOTTS. *Mr. and Mistress* by Heidi Betts is the story of millionaire Cullen Elliott and his mistress who is desperately trying to hide her unexpected pregnancy. Also out this month is the second book of Maureen Child's SUMMER OF SECRETS. *Strictly Lonergan's Business* is a boss/assistant book that will delight you all the way through to its wonderful conclusion.

We are launching a brand-new continuity series this month with SECRET LIVES OF SOCIETY WIVES. The debut title, *The Rags-To-Riches Wife* by Metsy Hingle, tells the story of a working-class woman who has a night of passion with a millionaire and then gets blackmailed into becoming his wife.

We have much more in store for you this month, including Merline Lovelace's *Devlin and the Deep Blue Sea,* part of her cross-line series, CODE NAME: DANGER, in which a feisty female pilot becomes embroiled in a passionate, dangerous relationship. Brenda Jackson is back with a new unforgettable Westmoreland male, in *The Durango Affair.* And Kristi Gold launches a three-book thematic promotion about RICH AND RECLUSIVE men, with *House of Midnight Fantasies.*

Please enjoy all the wonderful books we have for you this month in Silhouette Desire.

Happy reading,

Melissa Jeglinski

Melissa Jeglinski
Senior Editor
Silhouette Books

Please address questions and book requests to:
Silhouette Reader Service
U.S.: 3010 Walden Ave., P.O. Box 1325, Buffalo, NY 14269
Canadian: P.O. Box 609, Fort Erie, Ont. L2A 5X3

HEIDI BETTS

Mr. and Mistress

Published by Silhouette Books

America's Publisher of Contemporary Romance

Special thanks and acknowledgment are given to
Heidi Betts for her contribution to THE ELLIOTTS miniseries.

For Jackie Stephens—thanks for your help with the
research for this book, and for all the great e-mail chats!

And always, for Daddy.

 SILHOUETTE BOOKS

ISBN 0-373-76723-4

MR. AND MISTRESS

Books by Heidi Betts

Silhouette Desire

Bought by a Millionaire #1638
Blame It on the Blackout #1662
When the Lights Go Down #1686
Seven-Year Seduction #1709
Mr. and Mistress #1723

HEIDI BETTS

An avid romance reader since junior high school, Heidi knew early on that she wanted to write these wonderful stories of love and adventure. It wasn't until her freshman year of college, however, when she spent the entire night reading a romance novel instead of studying for finals, that she decided to take the road less traveled and follow her dream. In addition to reading,writing and romance, she is the founder of her local Romance Writers of America chapter and has a tendency to take injured and homeless animals of every species into her central Pennsylvania home.

Heidi loves to hear from readers. You can write to her at P.O. Box 99, Kylertown, PA 16847 (an SASE is appreciated but not necessary) or e-mail heidi@heidibetts.com. And be sure to visit www.heidibetts.com for news and information about upcoming books.

THE ELLIOTTS

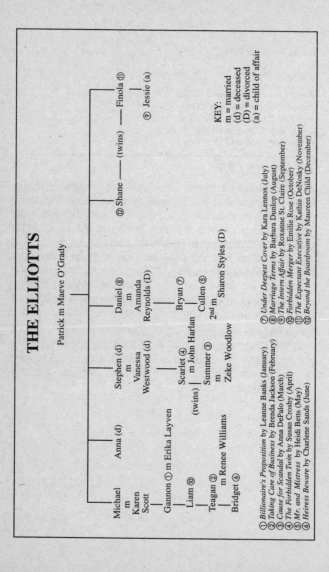

Patrick m Maeve O'Grady

Michael
m
Karen
Scott

Gannon ① m Erika Layven

Liam ⑩

Teagan ②
m Renee Williams

Bridget ⑥

Anna (d)

Stephen (d)
m
Vanessa
Westwood (d)

Scarlet ④
m John Harlan

(twins)

Summer ③
m
Zeke Woodlow

Daniel ⑧
m
Amanda
Reynolds (D)

Bryan ⑦

Cullen ⑤
2nd m
Sharon Styles (D)

⑫ Shane —— Finola ⑪
—— (twins)

⑨ Jessie (a)

KEY:

m = married
(d) = deceased
(D) = divorced
(a) = child of affair

① *Billionaire's Proposition* by Leanne Banks (January)
② *Taking Care of Business* by Brenda Jackson (February)
③ *Cause for Scandal* by Anna DePalo (March)
④ *The Forbidden Twin* by Susan Crosby (April)
⑤ *Mr. and Mistress* by Heidi Betts (May)
⑥ *Heiress Beware* by Charlene Sands (June)
⑦ *Under Deepest Cover* by Kara Lennox (July)
⑧ *Marriage Terms* by Barbara Dunlop (August)
⑨ *The Intern Affair* by Roxanne St. Claire (September)
⑩ *Forbidden Merger* by Emilie Rose (October)
⑪ *The Expectant Executive* by Kathie DeNosky (November)
⑫ *Beyond the Boardroom* by Maureen Child (December)

One

"Hello?"

"I'm in town. Thought I might come over."

His voice reached through the telephone wire and slid down her spine like warm maple syrup on a cold winter's day, into every nook and cranny of Misty Vale's traitorous body.

"All right," she replied softly. "I'll be waiting."

She hung up and quickly began moving around the room, straightening magazines and throw pillows, dimming the lights before heading for her bedroom. Shedding her skintight bike shorts and sports bra, she slipped into a new black teddy she knew Cullen would love.

If it weren't for him, she probably wouldn't own

half as many pieces of fancy lingerie. But he liked the sheer, sexy stuff, and she liked wearing it for him.

She quickly pulled her long, wavy hair out of its ponytail holder and ran a brush through to fluff it up.

A second later, the doorbell rang. She hurried across the room, glancing around one last time to be sure everything was in order. And then her hand was on the chain, releasing it. On the knob, turning it.

"Hi."

He was leaning against the jamb, black hair glistening in the porch light, blue eyes sparkling with barely banked desire. She swallowed hard, wishing she knew how to settle the butterflies flitting around in her belly.

"Hi. Come on in," she said, stepping back to allow him entrance.

She closed the door and refastened the security chain, then turned to find him watching her like a hawk might watch a mouse just before swooping down and carrying it away.

He was dressed for business in charcoal gray slacks and a white dress shirt, both of which were slightly wrinkled from a long day of meetings and travel. His tie was silk, with pastel swirls that reminded her of a painting she'd seen once in an art gallery. It was pulled away from his neck and hung limply from the collar with the top two buttons undone. The jacket that matched his slacks was folded over one arm.

He looked tired, and as much as she wanted to

drag him straight to the bedroom, she thought he might need to relax a bit first.

"Do you want anything?" she asked, tipping her head in the direction of the kitchen at his back. "A glass of wine? Something to eat, maybe?"

With the flick of his wrist, his jacket fell to the floor and he was striding forward, his gaze focused intently on her face.

"Later," he growled in a low voice that sent every cell of her being into erotic overdrive. His arms wrapped around her and a second later, his mouth hovered above hers. "Right now all I want is you."

As always, his kiss scorched, setting her afire from head to toe. She buried her fingers in the hair at the nape of his neck, caressing his scalp. His lips moved over hers, sucking, biting. His tongue delved inside to lick and stroke.

Her breasts swelled beneath the satin material of her teddy, pressing against his solid, muscled chest. His hands ran along her spine, over her waist, and finally cupped her buttocks, pulling her into the evidence of his arousal. Misty moaned, holding him tighter and hitching a leg up to hook on the jut of his hip.

Tearing his mouth away, he breathed heavily against her cheek. "Bedroom. Now."

"Yes."

Bending slightly, he lifted her into his arms and strode with purpose across the living room. He knew the layout of her apartment as well as she did. Not surprising, since he'd bought the building for her three years ago, after an accident on stage had damaged her knee and ended her career as a showgirl on the Las Vegas Strip. Her dance studio was downstairs, and she lived above.

Cullen lived in New York, working hard for *Snap*—one of his family's many successful magazine ventures—but he visited Nevada as often as possible. And whenever he was in town, he spent the night with her…in her bed.

She lived for those nights. Waited for them, craved them, even though everything inside her told her it was wrong.

He was five years her junior, his family—the Elliotts—one of the wealthiest and most prominent in New York. They couldn't have been more different if they'd been born in opposite hemispheres.

But from the moment she'd seen him, standing backstage after one of her nightly performances, there had been something about him. Something that drew her, kept her connected to him no matter how many times she told herself they should call off their blazing red-hot affair.

Reaching the edge of the bed, Cullen laid her on the mattress and followed her down, covering her body with his own.

"I love this," he said, fingering the black fabric that barely covered her from chest to thigh. "But it has to go. I want you naked."

"You're the boss," she told him with a small smile.

One side of his mouth quirked up in sensual

amusement as his fingers slipped beneath the teddy's spaghetti straps, sliding them over her shoulders and down her arms. She moved to allow him to uncover her breasts and pull the garment down past her hips and thighs.

His beautiful blue eyes seared through her like laser beams. He openly admired her breasts, her belly, the triangular area between her legs hidden behind a swatch of black lace.

Rising up from the bed, she helped him remove the lingerie completely. He tossed it aside, returning his attention to her bare, curvaceous form.

She wiggled anxiously, wanting to touch him. Wanting him to touch her.

"You're overdressed," she told him, grabbing the end of his tie and giving it a tug. The action brought him several inches closer, until their noses nearly touched.

His chest rose and fell with his harsh breathing and she took a moment to run her hands over the wide planes of his pectoral muscles before her fingers moved up to the knot at his throat.

She loosened the tie, taking her time pulling the length of silk free of his pristine white collar. Then she went to work on the buttons of his shirt, slipping them through their holes one by one. When she reached the bottom, she tugged the tails out of the waistband of his slacks, revealing his smooth, tanned chest and six-pack abs.

She swallowed, overwhelmed by the sheer perfection of Cullen's toned build. He'd mentioned once that he worked out several times a week in the company gym of Elliott Publication Holdings (EPH).

And she reaped the benefits.

Pushing the soft cotton off his shoulders, she pitched the shirt in the direction of her discarded negligee. Next came his belt, unbuckled and pulled through the loops of his pants. When her painted, manicured nails dipped behind the button at his waist, he sucked in a breath, sending his stomach rippling.

"I hope you're enjoying yourself," he said through gritted teeth, "because I fully intend to repay the favor."

"Uh-oh. I'm in real trouble, then, because I *am* enjoying myself. Very much."

She flicked the button of his trousers open with her thumb, creating even more space for her fingers to delve and explore. The heat of his body—so close to the throbbing, insistent center of him—enveloped her, soaking through her skin and down into her soul.

With the backs of her fingers brushing over the sprinkling of hair leading downward from his navel, Misty used the heel of her hand to push the zipper down. Slowly, the individual snicks echoed through the room.

Cullen held his breath, the sensations she was creating were almost too much to bear. Each click of the zipper teeth separating seemed to reverberate through his bones, his teeth, his rigid, straining shaft.

He'd been half-hard all day, anticipating the moment when he could tie up his *Snap* business in

Vegas and sneak away to make love to Misty. The things she was doing to him now didn't help matters, either. His blood was boiling, his head pounding. Much more, and he thought he might implode.

She was amazing. Every time they were together, it was like fireworks on the Fourth of July. Hot, vibrant, spectacular. He was surprised they hadn't set the sheets on fire years ago.

If he told anyone, even his brother, how Misty made him feel in bed, they would have given him one of those sly, knowing looks and said, "Sure. She used to be a showgirl. What do you expect?"

But it was more than that, because as explosive as they were in the bedroom, they worked just as well out of it. He wanted to make love to her as often as his schedule and physical endurance would allow, but he was equally happy to sit on the sofa with her and watch a movie or pick at day-old Chinese takeout.

That's what no one would have understood. What he didn't particularly understand himself.

The zipper reached its end and Misty dipped her entire hand into his pants, into his briefs to circle his pulsating length. His diaphragm seized, and his nostrils flared as he fought to pull air into his lungs. She stroked him, squeezed him, teased him until he wanted to scream.

"Enough." Before he lost it to her fingers instead of inside her where he most wanted to be, he grabbed her wrist and extracted her hand from his trousers.

In a few jerky moves, he kicked off his shoes, socks, pants and underwear.

Once he was naked, he climbed onto the bed, pushing her to her back as he straddled her thighs. Bracing his weight on his arms, he leaned forward and took her mouth the way he'd fantasized all through the long flight from New York.

She responded as she always did—passionately, with her whole heart and soul. Her arms wrapped around his neck and he sank down on top of her, luxuriating in the feel of her soft breasts pillowed against his chest.

Shifting beneath him, she somehow maneuvered so that his legs were no longer bracketing her. Instead, hers were now locked at the small of his back. He could feel her heels digging into his buttocks the same as her nails were digging into his shoulders.

He liked it. Maybe too much. Although, with Misty, it didn't seem to be a case of too much, but never enough.

Tugging at her bottom lip with his teeth, he broke their earth-shattering kiss and blazed a hot, damp trail down her body. He skimmed the slope of her throat, the rise of one breast, stopping to explore the tight bud of her nipple. He circled the areola with his tongue, then closed his mouth over the tip and began to suckle.

Misty writhed beneath him, making those sexy little mewling sounds in her throat that drove him crazy.

All day, he'd imagined the things he would do to her once he could break away and get to her apartment...the things she would do to him. But now that he was here with her, both of them naked and mindless and desperate, he didn't think he had the patience for any of them. He was hard and throbbing and simply wanted to sink himself inside her, then stay that way forever.

Lifting his head, he gazed down at her, chest heaving, blood rushing through his veins like a forest fire.

"I can't wait," he grated. "I'm sorry. I'll make it up to you, I promise."

And then he was thrusting inside her, buried to the hilt. Their gasps mingled as sensations washed over them, the friction almost too much to bear.

"Cullen," Misty panted, her fingers raking across his back, sure to leave marks. "Wait. We didn't use protection."

For a second, her words didn't make sense. He could barely hear her over the rushing in his ears. She felt amazing, so warm and wet and tight around him. Better than ever, if that was even possible.

Then suddenly what she was trying to tell him sank in.

He'd forgotten the condom. Dammit.

He pulled out immediately, shaking his head in disbelief. "I'm sorry, Misty. I don't know what's wrong with me. I've never been that careless before, I swear."

She smiled gently, wiggling out from under, then turned over and shimmied across the lavender coverlet toward the nightstand. "It's all right. I'm sure we caught the mistake in time. I don't think there's any need to worry."

He didn't reply, but hoped to hell she was right. It wasn't like him to forget something as important and ingrained as protection.

His eyes remained glued to her bare back, bottom and legs while she opened the top drawer of the bedside table, rooting around for a loose foil packet.

Such a close call should have cooled his ardor. Should have, but didn't. His mouth was still dry with wanting her.

She came back, crawling the few feet to the end of the bed, the shiny square held up between two fingers. "Got it," she said, her grin widening triumphantly.

Tearing one edge open with her teeth, she removed the latex circle and tossed away the empty wrapper. His eyes were riveted to her slim fingers as she held the condom lightly in both hands and slid it competently—mind-numbingly—down his rigid length.

He held his breath the entire time, afraid that if he moved, if he didn't hold completely, absolutely still, he would lose control and embarrass himself. His abdomen was concave with the effort not to inhale, his arms and legs shaking with the desire to reach out, topple her to the bed and simply take her. Ravish her.

She brought out the animal in him, no question. With any other woman, he would have tried to temper his response, hold back his natural instincts. But with Misty, he could do anything and know she was right there with him. Her passions matched his own, and she was daring enough to try anything once.

"Two seconds," he rasped, clenching his fists to keep from grabbing her.

Her brows drew together in confusion.

"That's how long you've got before I lose my patience and take over."

"Uh-oh. I guess I'd better make the most of the time I have left."

Rather than backing off, she drifted closer until they were thigh to thigh, chest to chest. She placed an openmouthed kiss on his chin, nipping lightly with her teeth as her lips slid away.

"One," she murmured.

Her fingers wrapped around the base of his erection and she gave a little squeeze, sending pleasure skyrocketing through every cell and nerve ending of his body.

"Two."

Before she could count to three or do anything else that threatened to send him over the edge, he grasped her wrists, lifted them above her head and leaned forward, toppling them both to the mattress. They bounced slightly, and Cullen found Misty's brief giggle infectious.

Still grinning, he crushed his mouth down on hers, at the same time running his palms down her body, over her arms, breasts, waist, hips. When he reached her thighs, he nudged them apart and settled more securely, hovering just above her feminine warmth.

With a single forward thrust, he sank inside, then froze, waiting for the ripple effect of the nearly knee buckling sensations to subside. His heart pounded hard in his chest, threatening to break through his rib cage.

Beneath him, Misty squirmed and moaned, raking her nails across his back and tilting her hips in an effort to drive him even deeper. He didn't think it was possible, but he was happy to let her try.

Bending her knees, she hugged his waist with her legs, and he began to move. At first his strokes were long and slow, as he took his time to enjoy the clasping heat of her moist sheath. But after only a minute or two, he knew he wouldn't last and began to increase his pace.

"Yes. Cullen, yes."

Misty's soft voice, mewling in his ear, sent flames licking through his bloodstream, heading straight for his groin.

"Misty." He breathed her name like a prayer, nipping at the tender spot between her neck and shoulder.

She cried out, arching her back and clenching around him as the waves of orgasm washed over her. He pumped his hips. Harder, once. Faster, twice. Stars burst behind his closed eyelids and he gave a guttural groan as everything inside him exploded.

"I should go."

Cullen's chest rumbled with the softly spoken words, jostling her awake just as she'd begun to drift off. She lay snuggled in his arms, her head on his shoulder, one arm draped across his stomach.

Stifling a sigh, she pushed away from him and sat up, keeping the sheet clutched above her breasts. She tucked a strand of hair behind her ear as she watched him sit up on the edge of the bed, then move around the room retrieving his clothes.

This was the part of their time together that she liked the least—when Cullen had to leave. He didn't always come over just to sleep with her and then take off. Sometimes he spent the night and they would have breakfast together in the morning. Once in a while, he even stayed for a few days and they would do normal everyday things together like watch television or take a walk in the park.

But no matter how long they were together, she hated to see him go. It made her heart hurt and emphasized the charade that was their relationship.

They were having an affair, that was all. They were never going to end up together, with a house and kids and a minivan in the driveway.

For one thing, she wasn't the minivan type. She was an ex-showgirl with bigger dreams and better taste. If she hadn't fallen on stage and ruined her knee three years ago, she would still be dancing in one of the flashy casinos on the Las Vegas Strip.

For another, Cullen wasn't the marrying type. He was twenty-seven to her thirty-two, but even if he weren't five years younger, he came from one of the wealthiest families in Manhattan. The likelihood of his wanting to spend the rest of his life with a woman like her—of his family ever *allowing* such a thing—was slim to not-a-chance-in-hell.

But the simple facts of the situation didn't keep her mind from making the occasional trip down fantasy lane, imagining what it might be like if she weren't an ex-showgirl/dance instructor and he weren't a high-powered magazine executive. If they were normal, everyday people who had met in some normal, everyday way.

She didn't spend long wishing for things that could never be, though. She was happy with her life, and happy with what she and Cullen had, even if she knew it wouldn't last.

For now, it was enough.

And she could certainly do worse…had done worse, considering some of the real treats she'd dated in the past. Compared to them, Cullen was a verita-ble Prince Charming.

In a tailored Italian business suit.

Dressed now, he stood at the end of the bed with his hands in his pockets. Scooting out from under the covers, Misty grabbed her silk robe from a hook on the back of the closet door and shrugged it on, looping the belt loosely at her waist.

"I'll walk you out."

He gave an almost imperceptible nod and they moved together through the living room area to the front door. She released the locks and turned the knob, but before she could open the door, Cullen stopped her with a hand on her wrist. When she lifted her head to meet his gaze, his eyes were smoldering.

Leaning in, he slid a hand under her hair to cradle her neck and kissed her until her bare toes curled. A full minute later, he pulled away and she clutched at the door to keep from melting into the carpet at their feet.

"If I didn't have to get back to New York by morning," he murmured softly, rubbing her bottom lip with the pad of his thumb, "I'd drag you back to bed and keep you there for a week."

"If you didn't have to be back in New York by morning," she whispered in return, "I'd let you."

One corner of his mouth lifted in a subtle grin and his arm dropped to his side as he stepped through the doorway, onto the landing above the stairwell that led to the alley at the back of her dance studio.

"I'll call you."

She nodded, then stood at the top of the stairs as she always did to watch him walk away.

Two

Four months later—late April

The music from the studio sound system, mixed with the staccato beat of her students' feet on the hardwood floor, pounded through Misty's head, making her wonder if she'd manage to stay on her feet.

For months now, she'd been fighting dizziness, nausea and a laundry list of other symptoms associated with the early stages of pregnancy. She'd thought, with the first trimester out of the way, that she might start to feel better. Instead, she felt worse.

Today was especially bad. She'd barely been able to get out of bed, and ever since had been fighting waves of lightheadedness and the need to lie down.

But she had classes to teach, and if she missed even one, her plan to become self-sufficient and support herself on the income from her dance studio would be in jeopardy.

Three years ago Cullen had bought this building in Henderson, just outside Las Vegas, for her and had it completely refurbished, turning the downstairs into a studio large enough to teach both children and adults.

As much as she'd hated taking his charity, he'd insisted, and the condition of her knee at the time hadn't given her much choice. It was either accept Cullen's generosity or risk being homeless in a matter of weeks.

But she'd promised him—and herself—that she would pay him back. Every cent, once the studio became profitable.

Unfortunately, that had yet to happen. What she made on her classes went for the little things like food and electricity, but Cullen was still paying for the general upkeep of the building and business.

She hated that, hated feeling like a kept woman, a mistress, even though that was exactly what she was.

It wasn't her affair with him that made her uneasy, but the fact that he was supporting her financially. It felt too much like he was leaving money on the night-stand for services rendered.

She didn't have much choice, though, did she? The only way to get out from under the debt she owed Cullen was to make a success of the studio, and with a baby on the way, that was suddenly more important than ever. Especially since Cullen had no idea he was going to be a father in five more months.

Resting a hand over her slightly distended abdomen, she swallowed past the dizziness that seemed to be with her twenty-four/seven these days, along with the sense of guilt she felt more often than not at keeping her pregnancy a secret from Cullen.

It was better this way, she reminded herself. If Cullen knew about the baby, he would want to do the right thing. He would insist they get married, even though it was the last thing he really wanted.

He'd been raised to always be responsible and protect the family name. When his father had gotten his mother pregnant right out of high school, his grandfather had insisted they marry to give the child a name and keep from tarnishing the family's sterling reputation.

Misty didn't want to put Cullen in that position, didn't want to force him into a situation he would hate and later resent her for.

No, it was better this way. She'd been avoiding him for months, ever since the home pregnancy test—and later a blood test at the doctor's office— had confirmed her suspicions.

If only she could avoid him a while longer, until the studio began to operate on its own funds, everything would be all right. She would be able to begin paying him back all the money he'd invested in her, and he would eventually come to realize that his unanswered and unreturned calls meant she didn't want to see him anymore.

She hated to break things off with him so abruptly, but it was best for everyone.

He'd been good to her. Better, she'd often thought, than a girl like she deserved. Because of that, and because she really did care for him, she refused to saddle him with a wife and a child he probably didn't want and had never planned for.

Misty pushed herself away from the mirrored wall where she'd been standing—leaning, more like—as the music drew to an end and the dancers' steps slowed. She was only half paying attention, she realized, but at least she'd been watching closely enough to know the routine had gone off with barely a hitch. This was her adult class, so they caught on more quickly than the children.

"Good job, guys," she told them, clapping her hands together in approval. "Now this next time through, I'd like you to add…"

Her words trailed off as the room started to spin around her. She'd only taken one step toward the line of women who were awaiting her instructions, but her heart was beating as if she'd run a mile. Her mouth went suddenly dry and her skull felt ready to explode.

And then the floor seemed to tilt upward, closing in. Her vision narrowed into a tiny pinpoint of darkness, and she knew she was in trouble a tenth of a second before the world went dark.

* * *

Cullen sat in the Elliott family booth at his brother's restaurant. Une Nuit was Bryan's pride and joy. Located on Ninth Avenue, between Eighty-Sixth and Eighty-Seventh Streets in New York City, the trendy, very popular establishment specialized in French/Asian fusion cuisine and was often praised in reviews and articles alike for its daring menu. The low red lighting set a seductive cast to the black suede and copper décor.

At the moment, Cullen was sipping a cup of coffee—some fancy French creation Bryan was apparently trying out this week—and waiting for John Harlan to arrive for lunch.

They'd been friends forever, and after a game of golf on Saturday where John beat him by thirteen humiliating strokes, Cullen had started to think he might be willing to confide in his friend about the recent troubles he'd been having with Misty.

He wasn't sure he was ready to tell anyone about her, but since she wasn't answering his calls, and his feet were itching to fly out there and discover for himself what the hell was going on, he thought a little advice from a friend might not be out of the question.

If it hadn't been for this damn competition his grandfather, Patrick Elliott, had set up between his sons to decide who would take over as CEO of EPH upon his retirement, he likely would have flown out long before now. But he'd been so swamped with work, he'd barely gotten out of the office at all the past few months, let alone found enough time for a trip to Vegas.

"Can I join you?"

He turned his head, surprised to find his cousin Scarlet standing beside his booth. She was dressed in one of her usual outlandish outfits, but just like all the others, the bright colors and stylish design suited her flamboyant personality.

"Mmm." He looked past her, then back into her pale green eyes. "I'm expecting—"

"Me."

Harlan appeared, almost out of nowhere, and Cullen would have had to be blind not to notice the sudden nervousness emanating from his cousin's slender form.

"So, three for lunch, eh?" Stash, the restaurant's manager, asked in his cheerful French accent.

"No." Scarlet stumbled back a step, bumping into John. John caught her by the elbows, keeping hold of her a moment longer than Cullen would have expected for mere acquaintances.

Before he could ask or even speculate as to what was going on between his cousin and John Harlan, his cell phone rang. He glanced at the caller ID screen, his stomach turning over at the number on the lighted display.

It was Misty, calling from the dance studio phone.

He'd been trying for months to reach her. He'd left dozens of messages, but she'd never called him back.

It was just an affair. One he'd intended to break off years ago. But having Misty avoid him, suspecting she was doing so in the hopes of breaking things off with him…

He didn't like it. And for some reason, it made him even more desperate to talk to her, see her.

He flipped his phone open before the second chirp ended. "Hello?"

"Mr. Elliott?" a voice questioned tentatively from the other end of the line.

It wasn't Misty, after all. But how would someone else, someone from Misty's studio, get his private mobile number?

With a frown, he said, "Yes."

"Umm…"

The woman, whoever she was, sounded even more nervous than before.

"My name is Kendra. I'm one of Misty's dance students."

"Yes," he said again, still confused.

"Well, umm…there's been a bit of an accident, and your number was the first on her speed dial. We didn't know who else to call."

"What?" His voice rose and he sat up straighter in the black suede booth, leaning forward on the copper-topped table. His brain was stuck on the word *accident,* barely processing anything else the woman said. "What happened?"

"She collapsed during our class, and—"

"How is she?" he demanded.

"I'm not sure. We called an ambulance, but—"

"Where'd they take her?"

"St. Rose Dominican Hospital."

With a sharp nod meant more for himself than anyone else, he barked, "I'll be there as soon as I can. If you learn anything more, call me immediately at this number, do you understand?"

Once the woman agreed, he said a curt goodbye, snapped his phone shut and rose from the booth all in one swift motion.

"I can't stay."

"What's wrong?" Scarlet asked. "Who's hurt?"

"No one you know." No one his family even knew about.

Meeting John's gaze, he apologized to the man for wasting his time. "Sorry. I appreciate your coming, but I need to get to Las Vegas."

"No problem. Anything I can do?"

"I'll let you know," Cullen replied through tight lips, already heading for the door. "Thanks."

Due in large part to the Elliott family jet and the pilot's awareness of Cullen's desperation to reach Henderson, Nevada, as quickly as possible, he arrived at the hospital just over five hours later.

He burst through the emergency room doors and made a beeline for the nurses' station, demanding an update on Misty's condition and to be taken to her. The nurse on duty—apparently used to frantic and distraught loved ones—looked up Misty's name on the computer, then gave him a room number and pointed him toward the elevators.

He took it as a good sign that she'd been moved from the emergency room to a regular room. And the nurse hadn't mentioned anything about the Intensive Care Unit.

Then again, wouldn't it have been better for Misty to have been treated and released?

His nerves jangled as he rode the elevator up to the third floor, his pulse racing in fear. He stepped out the minute the doors slid open and grabbed a passing nurse.

"Misty Vale," he demanded. "I'm looking for Misty Vale."

The young brunette smiled and turned back the way she'd come, leaving him to follow. "I just checked on her. She's fine. Resting. Poor thing, she just overdid it, plain and simple. Working too hard, not getting enough rest. And a woman can't keep that up, not in her condition."

Cullen barely listened to the nurse's one-sided conversation. He barely cared what was wrong with Misty; he just wanted to see her, to know she was all right.

The nurse paused at a closed door, the narrow vertical window above the knob too small to see much inside.

"Don't you worry," the nurse said, patting his arm. "She and the baby are both fine."

Leaving him alone outside Misty's room, she turned and padded back down the hallway.

Baby?

His mind raced, his mouth growing dry.

Baby?

His breathing grew ragged and his palms, he noticed, had begun to sweat.

What baby?

He felt as though his brain was about to explode, his fear for Misty's health mixing now with the news that there was a baby.

Misty's baby.

His baby?

He shook his head, knowing nothing would make sense until he saw Misty with his own two eyes.

Twisting the knob, he pushed the door open and stepped quietly into the darkened room. A low watt fluorescent light was on over an empty bed, the privacy screen pulled to keep it from bothering the sleeping patient.

Cullen tiptoed across the squeaky clean floor until he could see Misty, lying pale against the stark white sheets, her brown hair with its blond highlights the only splash of color in the room. An I.V. tube was taped to the back of her hand and monitors flashed and beeped, tracking her condition.

But what caught his attention, what sent a cold chill snaking down his spine, was the slight bulge of her abdomen beneath the plain cotton sheet.

She and the baby are both fine.

She and the baby...

My God, Misty really was pregnant.

He swallowed hard, not knowing quite what to think as he moved closer to her bedside.

A part of him wanted to be angry with her. Angry that she'd been avoiding him for the past three months. Of course, now he knew why.

Angry that she hadn't told him when she'd discovered the pregnancy, whether it was his child or not. But it was hard to hang on to his anger when she looked so small and vulnerable.

Lifting a chair from the corner, he carried it closer and sat at her side, wrapping his fingers around her still hand. His gaze floated over her face, eyes closed, lips parted gently in sleep. Down to her breasts, which seemed a bit fuller than he remembered. Then on to her belly, where their child rested.

Was there ever really any doubt that it was his baby? No.

As easy as it might be for many men to jump to the conclusion that their pregnant lovers had been sleeping with someone else, Cullen didn't consider it a real possibility.

Throughout their affair, they'd agreed to keep things open. He had certainly dated his fair share of other women, and he knew Misty had gone out a few times, too.

But he didn't think she'd slept with other men in the time they'd been together. It wasn't arrogance on his part, merely his belief that he'd gotten to know Misty pretty darn well in the past four years.

If she'd been sleeping with someone else, she'd have either mentioned it or found it hard to look him in the eye on his frequent visits. After all, she spoke quite openly of the times she'd been asked out by the occasional man and had agreed to go to dinner with him.

Cullen, on the other hand, didn't share the details of his frequent exploits with her. For one thing, they didn't lead to sex as often as he let people believe.

His family was wealthy, its members well-known and easily recognized in the Manhattan area. And he was the playboy of the family, the one who always had a beautiful young woman on his arm.

He'd escorted models, actresses, centerfolds, lawyers, ad executives, boutique owners... You name it, he'd dated it. Just as was expected. And for the better part of his twenty-seven years, he thoroughly enjoyed that lifestyle.

But there hadn't been as many women lately as one might expect. More and more, he found himself distracted by thoughts of Misty. By the desire to be with her and no one else.

He would almost rather go without a woman on his arm—or in his bed—and wait to see her again than be surrounded by attractive, willing females twenty-four hours a day.

Keeping one hand curled tightly around hers, he slid his other along the sheet that covered her to rest on the mound of her tummy.

He felt her stir and tilted his head to meet her eyes. They were a darker green than usual, clouded with distress.

"Cullen," she whispered, her voice scratchy from disuse. "What are you doing here?"

"I heard you weren't feeling well. Thought I'd drop by with some chicken soup."

For a moment, the corners of her mouth tipped up in a grin, but the aura of concern never left her face.

"How are you feeling?" he asked, hoping to distract her.

She blinked, her glance sliding away for a brief slip of time and then back. "I've been better."

"Misty…" He waited until he had her full attention, then flexed his fingers over her stomach so she would have no doubt what he was talking about. "Why didn't you tell me?"

Her eyes filled with tears, and her lower lip trembled. Cullen fought the urge to jump to his feet and gather her into his arms. He wanted nothing more than to comfort her, tell her everything would be all right, but he needed to hear her answer first. Needed to know why she'd kept such a huge secret from him for so long.

"I'm sorry," she said. Her voice trembled and she sniffed once before continuing. "I didn't know how to tell you, and the last thing I wanted was for you to feel obligated."

"Obligated?" he repeated, struggling to keep any sign of irritation from slipping into his tone. "It is my child, isn't it?"

Misty's chest rose as she took a deep breath, her chin lifting a notch. "Yes."

He'd thought her response would bring a sense of relief, but instead he felt nothing. Because he'd *known*. He hadn't needed to ask.

With a sharp nod, he sat up a bit straighter in his chair. There was a lot more he needed to know, but she didn't look in any shape for an inquisition right now.

"It's all right," he told her, squeezing her fingers and brushing his other hand over her brow and through her hair. "We'll talk later. For now, you should rest."

She looked unconvinced, but didn't argue. And soon enough, her eyelids began to droop.

He stayed with her until she fell asleep, thanking God that she and the baby were okay, and trying to formulate a plan for what needed to happen next.

Consulting with the doctor was at the top of his list. He wanted to know exactly what had happened to send her to the hospital in the first place, along with any treatment or special instructions she might need to follow.

Next was to get her home. She would be more comfortable there, as would he.

And then, after those two things were taken care of, he could move on to the really difficult part of his plan.

Convincing Misty to marry him.

Three

Misty entered her apartment two days later, keenly aware of Cullen's arm at her waist. He'd been with her practically every second since he'd first arrived at the hospital—solicitous and concerned.

His dark blue suit was wrinkled after two full days of wear. He kept extra clothes at her place, but he apparently hadn't left her side long enough to drop by and change, though it wouldn't have taken more than half an hour. He'd eaten meals in the room with her, and any time she'd opened her eyes during the night, it was to find him slouched down in an uncomfortable visitor's chair, still keeping watch over her, even in sleep.

It hurt her to realize he was being so sweet and

selfless after she'd spent the last three months avoiding and lying to him.

The guilt hit her like a punch to the gut, causing her to miss a step and stumble slightly. Cullen was there in an instant, catching her up and holding her steady with his strong hands cupping her elbows.

"Easy," he warned, his voice soft and caring as he guided her the rest of the way to the living room sofa.

After easing her down onto the overstuffed cushions, he stepped back and laid the plastic shopping bag that held her personal items on the coffee table.

She'd found out from one of the nurses that he'd paid her to run out on her lunch hour and buy some new clothes for Misty to wear when she was released so she wouldn't have to leave in the tights and leotard she'd been wearing when she was admitted.

"The doctor said you need to rest," Cullen told her, shrugging out of his suit jacket and tossing it over the back of a nearby armchair. "That means you lie down here or in bed. Whatever you need, you let me know. Understood?"

She bit back a smile. This must be what he was like at the *Snap* offices—the confident, commanding executive others saw in the boardroom and at his family's company, Elliott Publication Holdings.

"Yes, sir," she responded with a two-fingered salute.

His brows drew together in a scowl, which only amused her more, but he'd been so good to her, she didn't want him to think she didn't appreciate everything he was doing for her.

Kicking off the sandals that were a touch too large for her, she drew her legs up and stretched out along the full length of the sofa.

Cullen was there, almost before she could blink, fluffing a throw pillow and situating it beneath her head. "Good?" he asked.

When she nodded, he stepped away again.

"What else do you need? Are you hungry? Would you like some toast and tea? Maybe a glass of milk?"

He rocked back on his heels, hands stuffed into the pockets of his rumpled slacks. His hair was mussed, separated in several different places as though he'd been running agitated fingers through the dark locks on a regular basis, and his jaw was shadowed with two days' growth of beard.

She'd really had him worried, and knew she owed him more of an explanation than their brief conversation her first night in the hospital had allowed. Which he'd been polite enough not to bring up again.

Shaking her head, she said, "I'm fine. You look like you could stand to shower and change clothes, though. Why don't you go get cleaned up? I'll stay right here until you're finished. I promise."

His face remained impassive, unconvinced. She smiled, relieved when his shoulders seemed to relax and his eyes softened.

He pulled his hands out of his pockets and scratched absently at his chest. "You sure?"

"I'm sure," she said, offering an encouraging nod.

"All right." He stuck around for another few

seconds, then turned resolutely on his heel and skirted around the living room furniture on his way to the bedroom and master bath.

For the next twenty minutes, Misty lay perfectly still, not tired, but confused knowing that she couldn't break her promise to remain where she was until he got back. Her head ached, and she didn't think it was from the exhaustion that had landed her in the hospital to begin with.

No, she was preoccupied and stressed because she had no idea how things between Cullen and her would play out.

She hadn't wanted him to know about the baby because she suspected he would have had one of two reactions. Either he would be appalled and go running in the opposite direction as fast as modern technology could carry him, or his huge responsibility streak would kick in and he'd insist on taking care of her and their child, at least financially.

She had no doubt he could afford to give this baby the best of everything. The best clothes, the best education, the best toys. Misty could never compete on the modest amount she made with the dance studio…that is, if Cullen allowed her to keep it.

And even though it frightened her to think such a thing, the fact remained that he had the wealth and power to take this child from her, if he so desired.

What if he decided he didn't want to be with *her* anymore, but did want the baby?

What if he decided he wanted the baby to be raised

in New York, with all the respectability and privilege he and his family could provide?

What if he didn't have a problem with the mother of his child being an ex-showgirl, but when he told his family about her and the child they'd conceived illegitimately, they threw a fit and insisted he bring the baby home—without her?

The possibilities rolled through her brain like a dust storm, each one worse than the last.

Cullen was a good man, one of the best she'd ever met. He didn't treat her like an ex-showgirl, which some men equated with an ex-stripper or ex-prostitute.

But their relationship had never exactly been normal. She was a kept woman, plain and simple. And that was okay with her; she'd always been all right with it.

Because she was also self-assured and self-reliant, she'd made a conscious decision to begin an affair with Cullen. To become his mistress.

Getting pregnant changed everything. The unwritten rules they'd established along the way no longer applied.

And while her heart told her Cullen was a decent, caring guy, her brain continued to warn that he was an Elliott. A big, rich, powerful Elliott…and as far as his family would be concerned, she was a big, fat nobody.

She was the daughter of a showgirl who'd grown up to be a showgirl herself. Which was exactly what she'd always wanted. From the time she was a little girl, growing up backstage at some of the most glamorous casinos on the Vegas Strip, all she'd ever wanted was to grow up and follow in her mother's sequined, stiletto shoes.

What she *hadn't* wanted was to end up married and divorced several times like her mother, who was currently on husband number four. Happily, having the time of her life, but Misty had still hoped to avoid that particular habit.

She also hadn't intended to be a single mother, but it looked like that was the future she'd mapped out for herself by hooking up with a man to become his mistress and managing to get herself pregnant in the process.

She groaned aloud at the entire mess.

"What's wrong?"

Cullen's deep worried voice from behind her made her jump and twist around on the couch.

"You scared me," she said, her hand over her heart, which was pounding against her rib cage.

"Are you okay?" he demanded, stalking forward.

"I'm fine."

"You moaned."

"Technically," she told him, "I groaned."

Shifting around until she was lying flat on her back, she cast her gaze downward and ran a hand over the swell of her belly, where their child rested. She'd felt it move already, fluttering around inside her womb, reminding her that it was a living being, soon to be kicking and crying and needing her to take the very best care of him or her.

"I was just thinking about what a mess I've made of things. That's groan-worthy, wouldn't you say?"

He came around, hair still dripping, and took a seat in the chair directly across from her. She didn't have to move a muscle in order to meet him eye-to-eye.

He was barefoot, wearing a pair of worn, comfortable jeans and a maroon polo shirt. It was one of his favorite outfits, and he wore it often when he stayed with her for more than a few hours.

It was one of her favorites, too. He looked approachable and normal, and whenever she saw it, she knew she'd have a bit more time with him.

"Don't be so hard on yourself. You weren't exactly alone in the process."

She lowered her gaze, not sure what to say to that.

"We should probably talk about it, don't you think?"

Taking a deep breath, she nodded. "I know you must have a lot of questions."

"I do." Leaning forward, he braced his forearms on his thighs and clasped his hands together. "How far along are you?"

"Sixteen weeks."

His eyes narrowed as his mind worked through the math. "That's four months. Right around the last time we were together."

She swallowed hard, inclining her head for fear anything she tried to say would come out as a strangled squeak.

"When did you find out?"

"About a month later."

A beat passed while he considered that, a slight tick pulling taut the skin of his newly shaved jaw.

"I guess that explains why you stopped taking my calls and never answered any of the messages I left."

"I'm sorry." Drawing herself into a sitting position, she stuffed the pillow against the arm of the sofa and leaned back. "I know that was terrible of me, but I was just so…confused. At first I didn't even believe it. We've always been so careful except for that one time we forgot to use a condom at first. But no matter how many of those home pregnancy tests I took, they all came out the same. Even after I saw the doctor, I think I was still in denial. And I knew that if we spoke, you'd notice something was going on just from the tone of my voice."

She sighed, linking her own fingers in her lap to keep from fidgeting. "I didn't want to lie and say nothing was wrong, so I took the coward's way out and said nothing."

"You were avoiding me?"

"Yes," she admitted, the word coming out breathy with guilt.

"Don't you think I had a right to know?"

The question vibrated with barely concealed anger, snaking around her spine and making her shiver.

"Of course you did. You had every right. My only excuse for not telling you as soon as I found out was that I was afraid. And, if you can believe it, I was trying to protect you."

"Protect me?" he scoffed, jumping to his feet and

beginning to pace. Those long tanned fingers drove through his hair before coming down to settle on his denim-clad hips.

"Yes," she said, with more passion than she had realized she felt on the issue. "Cullen, you're twenty-seven years old. You're an Elliott, the director of sales for one of your family's most successful magazines. You're too young to be tied down by a washed-up dancer with a bum knee and a child you never signed on for. Your family wouldn't thank you for the bad press such a relationship would bring if the media ever found out."

He'd stopped pacing and was now glaring at her hard enough to bore holes through her forehead.

"Do you think I give a *damn* about a few newspaper headlines?"

"Maybe not now," she cautioned, "but how will you feel later, when your family starts to blame you for the damage you've done to their sterling reputation by getting involved with someone like me?"

Cullen narrowed his eyes and consciously tried to unclench his teeth before they were gritted to nubs. He couldn't decide which was closer to the boiling point—his annoyance or his blood pressure.

He hated to hear her talk about herself that way, making an issue of the fact that she was older than he was and assuming his family would disapprove of her simply because she used to be a showgirl on the Las Vegas Strip.

Although, on that last point, she was probably

right. His grandfather, especially, would be livid if he came home with an ex-showgirl mistress and an illegitimate child.

But then again, when was Patrick Elliott ever content with his family's behavior? Nothing any of them did seemed to garner the old man's approval. Cullen, for one, was tired of trying.

And he knew the rest of the family probably felt the same. They didn't so much respect the elder Elliott as they gave him a wide berth and avoided his condemnation as much as possible.

"Someone like you, huh?" His teeth were still clenched so tightly they ached, and if Misty was paying attention, she'd realize just how close he was to the end of his rope.

But she didn't appear to notice. She simply looked up at him with those bright green, almond-shaped eyes that drew him like a moth to a flame.

"We both know I've always been just an amusing pastime for you," she replied quietly. "Our relationship was never meant to become permanent, and I won't change the rules on you now."

One…two…

His nostrils flared as he inhaled sharply.

Three…four…

In. Out.

Five…six…

Inhale. Exhale.

Seven…eight…

If he kept breathing, kept counting, maybe the

curtain of red that fluttered at the edges of his vision would dissipate and he would no longer feel such a strong urge to put his fist through the nearest wall.

Nine...ten...

"Number one," he forced himself to say in a calm, even voice, "you were not just an amusing pastime. I admit things started out hot and heavy between us, and we got involved mostly because the sex was great. But I can get sex at home; I don't need to fly nearly three thousand miles every couple of months for a good lay."

She cringed at his crude language, but didn't interrupt. Good thing, because even the pain of his nails digging into the palms of his fisted hands didn't lessen the fury roiling in his gut.

"Number two, regardless of what our relationship may or may not have been up to now, the rules *have* changed. You're pregnant with my baby, and whether you like it or not, that changes everything.

"Number three, I love my family. I would never do anything to deliberately hurt or embarrass them, but they don't dictate the direction of my life. I make my own decisions. Is that clear?"

Her tongue darted out to wet her dusky pink lips, and he had to remind himself to hold on to his anger instead of stalking over to the sofa and kissing her silly the way his wayward libido wanted him to.

"Is that clear?" he asked again, with just enough sting to hold her attention and draw his own focus back to the matter at hand.

She nodded. It wasn't the most self-assured gesture he'd ever seen her make, but it was enough.

"Good." He loosened the fists at his sides, flexing his fingers to return feeling to the tingling digits. "Because I've made a decision. Not for my family and not out of some misplaced sense of responsibility. For me."

He waited a beat and then told her flat out, "We're getting married."

The color washed from her face until she was paler than she'd been when he'd first walked into her hospital room.

She gasped, her hand at her throat. "Cullen—"

"No," he said, cutting her off. Moving to the chair he'd occupied earlier, he perched on its edge and leaned toward her. "Don't argue, just listen. I want this baby, Misty. It's my child, as much a part of me as it is a part of you. I've already missed the first four months of your pregnancy—I don't want to miss any more. I want to be there every step of the way. I want to rub your feet when your ankles swell, bring you pickles and ice cream at three in the morning and hold your hand during the delivery. More importantly, I want to see the baby every day, not just on weekends or whenever I can manage to fly out here. And the best way to do that is for us to get married."

"Cullen—"

"Marry me, Misty."

Her eyes never left his, and he could have sworn he saw the glitter of tears along her lower lashes. His heart stuttered in his chest, and his mouth went dry as he awaited her answer.

Who could have known doing the right thing, laying claim to his child, would be so damned nerve-racking?

He watched her lips part, begin to move, but nothing could have prepared him for her answer when it finally came.

"I'm sorry, Cullen, I can't."

Four

Misty's heart broke a little more with each word she uttered, her stomach churning as she saw the impact they had on the man sitting across from her. His lips flattened and his expression turned stony.

She was hurting him, when that was the last thing she ever wanted to do. Didn't he understand? Didn't he realize that marrying her would ruin him?

She would step in front of a bus before she'd ever knowingly do anything to cause Cullen pain or humiliation. And whether he realized it or not, marrying her was a one-way ticket to both.

Besides, no matter what Cullen said, she didn't believe his deep sense of duty played no part in his offer. She knew perfectly well that Bryan, his brother, was the result of an unplanned pregnancy. His father had gotten his mother pregnant at age eighteen, and Cullen's grandfather had forced them to marry. But after twelve years of marriage and two children, they'd divorced.

Misty didn't want that for herself or for her child. And she didn't want Cullen sacrificing his happiness and future because of the guilt and responsibility that had been drilled into him from childhood.

She implored him with her eyes to recognize where she was coming from. "Please don't be angry, Cullen. It's a very sweet offer, and I know you're doing what you think is best, but I won't marry you just because the condom broke or we got a little careless."

Resting a splayed hand on her belly, she told him, "I want this baby, too. I'll be a good mother, and you don't ever have to worry that I'll deny you custody or any of your rights as a father. I would never do that."

He studied her for long minutes like a bug under a microscope. Her pulse quickened and she found herself squirming nervously at his close scrutiny. She couldn't even begin to guess what he was thinking or what his response might be.

"Have you given any thought to the doctor's instructions?" he asked finally, obviously struggling to control his emotions. "If you're not careful, you'll wind up back in the hospital—or worse, lose this baby."

At the very thought, a cold chill whipped through her. She wrapped both arms around the innocent life resting safely in her womb and hunched over slightly, her protective instincts already kicking in.

"I won't lose this baby," she said, and it was both a promise and a prayer.

"You will if you keep pushing yourself. The doctor said you collapsed from exhaustion and dehydration. The student from your class who called to tell me you were being rushed to the emergency room said you've doubled up on some of your classes and had extra ads put in the local papers to drum up more business."

"I may have overdone it a bit," she admitted, "but I won't let it happen again."

The blue of his eyes flashed briefly like sapphires under glass. "Why were you doing it at all?"

There it was, the sixty-four thousand dollar question. She took a deep breath, then slowly exhaled.

"You know as well as I do that the studio is struggling. With a baby on the way, I thought it would be prudent to get as much money as possible coming in before I have to stop teaching altogether. Lord knows I can barely support myself right now, let alone a child. I don't even have enough to hire someone to come in and cover for me during the last few months of my pregnancy, until I can get back to teaching the classes myself."

"You think I wouldn't support my own child?" he growled, his brows snapping together in fury. "I've been supporting you well enough for the past three years. Did you expect me to suddenly cut you off because I found out you were pregnant?"

She sighed. As hard as she'd tried to avoid it, she'd managed to bring his anger at her back full throttle.

Sliding off the sofa, she crawled on her knees across the soft beige carpet to his side. She wrapped her arm around one of his legs, her fingers resting on his strong upper thigh.

"Of course not," she replied quietly. "I didn't mean it like that. But, Cullen, I can't keep letting you pay my bills forever. I appreciate everything you've done for me. God knows what would have happened to me after my knee injury if it hadn't been for you. But I told you from the very beginning that I would pay back every penny of the start-up costs you put into buying this building and renovating it so I could live and hold classes here. Not to mention the money you put into my checking account every month, since the studio is still operating in the red."

She frowned at that. If anything, the monthly stipend bothered her more than his setting her up to teach dance classes. It reminded her too vividly of her own inability to fully support herself, of her dependency on a man to put a roof over her head and food on the table, and of the true nature of her relationship with Cullen.

She was his mistress, and for all intents and purposes, he was her benefactor. It was a hard truth to swallow.

"I've told you before you don't have to repay me. It wasn't a loan, it was a gift."

"Hell of a gift," she muttered, only half under her

breath. She knew for a fact he'd put more than a hundred thousand dollars into helping her get the studio up and running, and that didn't include the generous chunk of money sitting in her bank account, earning interest even as they spoke.

"The point is," he said, stressing the words just enough to let her know he was changing the direction of the conversation, "you *aren't* going to be able to teach classes for much longer. You probably shouldn't be teaching at all, considering where it landed you the last time. And then what?"

She opened her mouth to speak, but he held up a hand to stop her and continued.

"I'm sorry, Misty, but I don't want to be a long-distance father. I don't want to be a long-distance father-to-be."

Her heart began to pound, her stomach rolling and pitching like an amusement park ride. "What do you want, then?"

He took a deep breath, his chest puffing out as air filled his lungs, and covered the hand she had on his leg with his own. His long fingers engulfed her much smaller ones, the heat of his palm soaking into her bloodstream warming every inch of her body.

"Come back to New York with me."

"What?" She sat back, startled. It was the last thing she'd expected to hear.

"Come to New York with me. You can't cancel classes and keep the studio open, but you can't continue teaching, either. And I know you, Misty.

Without something to do, you'll be bored out of your mind in a week."

He squeezed her hand, the simple action conveying the importance of his plea.

"So come to New York with me. It will be good for the baby. You need to rest, and my town house is quiet and comfortable. Plus, I'll be there to wait on you hand and foot."

For the first time, she felt a stirring of amusement. "Hand and foot, huh?"

A suggestive sparkle lit his eyes. He slid his fingers beneath her hand and turned it palm up before lifting it to his mouth.

"Hand," he whispered, pressing a kiss to the very center, "and foot."

He molded his lips to the tip of one finger, sucking it gently into his mouth. A tidal wave of desire washed over her, sending her insides quivering. If she hadn't already been sitting, heels propped against her bottom, she thought for sure she would have slid to the floor in a puddle of raw nerve endings.

"Misty?" he asked softly. "Are you listening?"

It took a moment for his words to sink in, and another moment to find her voice. Even then, all she could manage was a weak, "Mmm-hmm."

"Another reason I'd like you to fly back with me is to meet my parents. Now that they're going to be grandparents, I'd like you to get to know each other."

The haze of longing clouding her vision slowly

began to clear. His parents? He wanted her to meet his parents?

Dear God, she could just picture the introductions. *Mom, Dad, this is Misty, my pregnant ex-showgirl mistress.* Their eyes would bug out and their mouths would drop open…but only long enough for them to collect their wits and start in with the hostile glares at her and the lectures to Cullen about mixing his Elliott blue blood with that of a dancer of questionable breeding and obviously low morals.

She'd rather walk naked down the crowded Vegas Strip.

"Come on, Misty," he cajoled. "You owe me."

Her eyes widened. *"That's* what you expect in trade for everything you've done for me?" she asked, incredulous.

"I meant, you owe me a few considerations for keeping this baby a secret from me for the past four months."

Well, he had her there. But still…*meeting his parents?* Wasn't that a bit above and beyond?

"Besides," he went on, "it doesn't have to be forever. Consider it a short vacation. You can come back here any time you want."

Still holding her hands, he got to his feet, pulling her up beside him. He drew her close and she went willingly, because it was where she felt safest, most comfortable.

Being in his arms was like sinking into a warm, scented bubble bath after a long night of dancing under blazing hot stage lights in four-inch heels and a headdress that weighed as much as a small car. Only better.

"And you never know," he murmured next to her ear while he caressed the swell of her waist. "Maybe seeing where I live and meeting my family will change your mind about accepting my proposal."

Leaning back, she met his hopeful, expectant gaze and made her decision. For better or for worse, she did owe him something for keeping the pregnancy a secret for so long, and for all he'd done for her over the years—not the least of which was making her feel protected and special.

"I'll go with you to New York," she told him, and was rewarded with a wide smile that revealed a row of straight white teeth, as well as his pure, unadulterated happiness.

"But I won't marry you," she cautioned before he could get carried away. She waved a pointed finger under his nose for emphasis. "That's not part of the bargain."

His grin didn't waver as he lowered his head and covered her mouth with his own. "We'll see."

Once Misty had agreed to accompany Cullen back to Manhattan, he wasted no time putting the wheels in motion.

He called the pilot of his family's private jet to let him know they would be wanting to leave first thing in the morning, made arrangements for someone to take over the classes at her studio, then carried Misty to the bedroom and deposited her on the mattress near the headboard, pillows propped behind her back.

No matter how much she protested that she was well enough to pack her own bag, he wouldn't hear of it. She had to sit there, watching and talking him in the right direction as he pulled her suitcase out of the closet and proceeded to fill it.

She didn't know whether to laugh or cringe at the way he stuffed her things together without folding, without giving a thought to the fact that the heels of her shoes might snag the delicate fabric of her skirts and blouses. When she pointed it out, he made a valiant effort to fix the problem, but eventually gave up, telling her that he would replace anything that got damaged in transit.

And even though they'd been sleeping together for four years, sharing the intimacies of a married couple, she was amazed to find that she still blushed to see him sorting through her lingerie drawers. He seemed to take great pleasure in picking which items she would take with her to New York, waggling his eyebrows and leering until she doubled over in laughter.

When he was finished, he zipped the suitcase closed and set it aside, then helped her change for bed. Climbing in beside her, he stroked her hair and held her until they both drifted to sleep.

The next morning, they drove to the airstrip in his rental car, and five hours later landed on the East Coast.

The trip passed with surprising ease, a thousand

times more comfortable and quiet than a commercial flight would have been. Cullen even made sure there was food on board so she would have a meal before they landed.

But everything about the posh plane and Cullen's solicitousness only served to remind her of how very out of place she would be in his world. She didn't need to worry about how long she could stand to stay with him at his Upper West Side town house. After a week, he and his family would likely be begging her to leave and forget she'd ever heard the Elliott name.

She'd slept on the plane, so by the time they arrived at his place, she was wide awake and practically shaking with nerves. Why she was so anxious about simply seeing where he lived, she wasn't sure.

A part of her expected to find a brood of Elliotts on the other side of the door, their eyes filled with condemnation, ready to attack. Another part of her thought it was probably the simple act of moving in with him—even for the short term—that had her palms shaking and her knees quaking.

He wanted her to meet his parents. He wanted to be an active participant in the remainder of her pregnancy and in their child's life. That all felt entirely too…domestic to her. Too much as though once she dipped her toes into the pool of his personal life, she would never be able to get out.

It might be a step up for her, but not for Cullen, and she had no intention of dragging him down. If he married her, he would become a laughingstock within his circle of friends, not to mention lose the respect of his peers at EPH and in the business world.

No, she would never put him in such a position. She cared too much about him.

He helped her out of the luxurious black Town Car he'd arranged to have pick them up at the airport, then scooped her into his arms and carried her up the front steps of his well-maintained brownstone.

Setting her on her feet, he dug his keys out of his pocket, then took her hand and led her inside, leaving the door open for the driver to follow with their bags. When that was done, he tipped the man and locked the door again after seeing him out.

He turned back, his mouth curled in a soft smile, his fingers buried in the front pockets of the same jeans he'd worn at her apartment.

"I like your house," she told him, glancing around a second time at her surroundings.

It was obvious someone of considerable wealth lived here, but the place wasn't quite as opulent as she'd expected. Instead, what she could see looked useful and lived-in.

The floors were hardwood, polished to a glossy sheen. Large rooms sat off to either side of the doorway and small foyer.

One was a living room area, complete with a large-screen plasma television, black leather sofa and chairs and a stereo on the shelves along the far wall.

The other room seemed to be Cullen's home

office. A desk stood at the far end of the room, complete with a computer, phone and lamp. The wall shelving on this side of the house was filled with books of all shapes and sizes, and there was even a window seat facing the street where a person could curl up to read on a rainy afternoon.

"Thanks," Cullen said, coming up behind her and curling his hands over her bare shoulders. "I want you to consider this your house, too. Make yourself at home. Snoop around, if you want, so you know where everything is. And if there's anything you need, don't be afraid to ask."

She nodded slightly, but knew she would only ever feel like a guest here.

"Are you tired?" he asked, rubbing the nape of her neck with the pads of his long, strong fingers.

"Not really," she answered, but she couldn't help moaning at the bone-melting sensations he was creating with his talented hands. Her head fell forward and her eyes slid shut.

"In that case, why don't we get you unpacked and settled in?"

His arms dropped back to his sides and he took a step away. She straightened, biting back a moan at the loss of his mesmerizing attentions.

"Then maybe we can crawl into bed," he added.

"I told you, I'm not very tired. I slept on the plane."

One black brow winged upward and a devilish glint lit his blue eyes. "Who said anything about sleeping?"

Five

Cullen sat at the foot of his bed, listening to the sounds of Misty moving around in the bathroom. Every few seconds, he caught a glimpse of her as she set something on the sink or rearranged his toiletries to make room for her own bottles and jars.

It had taken him half the night to convince her to unpack fully and make herself at home, rather than leaving her clothes in her suitcase or in only one drawer, and her makeup and beauty items in their case on the nightstand.

Now she was putting things where they would be if she lived here, but she was doing it reluctantly.

He drew a deep breath and rubbed the lines

forming across his brow. This was going to be more complicated than he'd thought.

Misty and the baby belonged with him. He wanted them in his house, in his life…but he wanted them to *want* to be there.

From the expression on Misty's face every time he made a remark about incorporating her into his home or family, he wasn't sure that would ever happen.

The noises from the master bath died down and he lifted his head to find Misty standing in the doorway. She looked nothing like the woman he'd first seen on that Las Vegas casino stage four years ago.

Then, she'd worn a skimpy, sequined costume that showed off all of her hot feminine assets to perfection and caught his attention faster than a flare gun being fired next to his ear.

Now, she looked like a PTA mother or Manhattan socialite—the sexy kind that got every man's temperature rising and every woman sharpening her claws. And he should know; he'd known his fair share of both.

If she thought she wouldn't fit in with his family, with his lifestyle, or just here in New York, she was wrong. Misty could fit in anywhere in the world, primarily because she was the type of woman who forced the world to conform to her instead of the other way around. Vibrant, beautiful, self-assured. Except for this moment, when she looked nervous and unsure.

Pushing off the bed, he rose to his feet and took two steps in her direction. "Everything okay?"

She nodded, but her teeth worrying her lower lip belied the motion.

"I think so. I'm not sure you'll like where I put everything. I had a lot of stuff and had to move some of your things around."

"I'm sure it's fine."

She cast a glance over her shoulder and Cullen rolled his eyes, deciding he had to do something or she'd fret herself sick the rest of the night.

"Come here, Misty," he said softly.

Her gaze turned back, landing on him. Without question, she drifted toward him, her pink low heeled slides nearly disappearing in the tall thick nap of his bedroom carpet.

As soon as she was close enough, he reached out and engulfed her in both arms, pulling her snug against his chest. "Don't be nervous," he whispered into her hair. "You belong here. With me."

She didn't respond, but he felt the shudder roll through her body. He pressed a kiss to her temple, then her cheek, then her lips, a burst of pleasure filling his chest as she opened her mouth beneath his.

His fingers wound through her hair, holding her in place as their tongues parlayed. Every dormant hormone flared to life and started coursing through his bloodstream like a forest fire.

It had been four months. Four long, dry months when he'd dreamed of Misty, fantasized about taking her to bed, but had been unable to do so because she'd been avoiding his phone calls, hiding her pregnancy from him.

He waited for anger or annoyance or a need for revenge to rear its ugly head, but he felt nothing along those lines. Only lust and a protective instinct so sharp it nearly crippled him.

His hand slid down the line of her body, coming to rest on the mound of her belly. On his child.

He lifted his head, breathing heavily. "I want to make love to you, but I don't want to hurt you."

"You won't," she said, her voice thin and feathery.

With his left hand cupping her stomach, he brought his right hand around to cradle her face. "But I've never made love to you before while you were pregnant, and you just got out of the hospital."

She mimicked his posture, putting one hand at his waist and placing the other along his jaw. "I was in the hospital because I wasn't careful enough with my health, not because there was something wrong with the baby. They kept me there until they were sure I was okay, and you've taken excellent care of me ever since. You won't even let me walk around on my own, if you're there to carry me," she added with a teasing grin. "I'm fine. And I want you to make love to me."

His gut clenched until he thought he might double over with the impact her words had on him. She had humbled him, while at the same time making him feel like the most powerful man in the world. She treated him like a hero…her hero, and damned if he didn't want to be one for her.

He released her long enough to walk around the bed and fold back the covers, dimming the lights while he was there. When he returned to her side, he tipped her head back and kissed her, letting her know how much he wanted her, how he felt about her.

At the same time, they began to slowly undress. His hands slipped beneath the hem of her sweater, luxuriating in the silken smoothness of her waist as he pushed the top upward. Her fingers fiddled with the buttons at the front of his shirt, loosening them one by one.

Raising her arms, she allowed him to strip the top up and over her head. As soon as she was free of the garment, she returned the favor by running her hands over his bare chest and pushing his shirt off his shoulders. Her touch raised trails of blazing heat beneath his skin, causing his breath to catch.

She pressed her lips to the hollow at the base of his throat and Cullen had to clench his fists to keep from throwing her down on the bed and taking her like some hardened criminal newly released from prison.

He focused his attention instead on the front closure of her robin's-egg blue slacks, shucking them down her legs and letting her use his shoulders for balance while she stepped out of them, leaving her shoes on the carpet, as well.

Straightening once again, he took in her tall lush form. She was only a few inches shorter than his own six foot one, and she'd always been curvy enough to make a grown man weep.

But now, four months into her pregnancy, she looked positively mouthwatering. One part Madonna, one part sex kitten. Cullen wondered what he'd done in his life to deserve such a gift.

Beneath the lacy cups of her demure white bra, her breasts were larger than before, but it was her belly that drew his gaze. His child rested inside that hard, half-a-basketball-size mound.

Dropping to his knees, he settled his hands on either side of her waist, then leaned forward to press his lips to her taut skin. He had the sudden, inane urge to talk to the little life on the other side. To say hello and tell his child he couldn't wait to meet him or her. To promise his unconditional love and protection.

Instead, he tilted his face up, meeting her emerald eyes. "What does it feel like?" he asked in a low tone. "To be pregnant?"

For a minute, he thought she might laugh at such a ridiculous question. He should have known better. Misty would never mock another person's sincere, heartfelt emotions.

The tips of her fingers feathered his hair as she looked down at him, a small smile playing on her lips. "What part?" she wanted to know. "The morning sickness? The tender, enlarged breasts? Or the bizarre midnight cravings?"

"Everything. I want to know everything."

Still on his knees, he turned her until her back was to the bed, then shifted her around to sit on the end of the mattress. It wasn't easy to stay where he was, but he needed to hear this, needed to know what he'd missed.

"The morning sickness wasn't fun. I suffered with that from the moment I woke up in the morning until mid-afternoon every day for the first three months."

She made a face and the corners of his lips tugged upward.

"My breasts are getting bigger," she told him with a pointed look at her chest, "but I imagine you'll enjoy that. And they are tender, but not unbearably so. Just be careful."

He nodded. She didn't need to worry about that. She already felt like a porcelain doll in his big hands. He had no intention of doing anything that would hurt or even discomfort her.

"The cravings have been interesting. I've been told they'll get worse the farther along I am, but I've already found myself starving for strange things like asparagus and maraschino cherries." She lowered her gaze, her cheeks turning an attractive shade of pink. "And there was one time that I raided an all-night convenience store for powdered donuts. I bought every box they had of both the regular size and the minis, then went home and ate them all with about six glasses of milk while I watched re-runs of *I Love Lucy.*"

He chuckled, imagining the sight of her curled up on the couch amidst an avalanche of white powder, and wished he could have been with her. Wished he could have been the one to run out at 3:00 a.m. to find whatever odd food item she was hungry for at that particular moment.

"What about the baby? How does it feel to have a brand-new life growing inside you?"

She licked her lips, her breasts rising as she drew a deep breath. "Do you really want to know?" she asked.

More than anything. "Of course."

"Terrifying."

His brows knitted in a frown. That wasn't at all the sort of answer he'd expected.

"Every day," she continued, "I wake up to find something else changed about my body. My breasts will be larger, my stomach will be rounder, my hands or ankles will be swollen. And then there's the thought of how little the baby is."

She splayed her hands over her middle, covering his own hand that still rested there.

"I know it's growing more every day, but it's still just a tiny, completely helpless being, relying on me to take care of it for nine whole months. I worry about everything I put in my mouth. About how much sleep I get, the shoes I wear, if I'm sitting too close to the television…"

Her expression turned earnest and she clutched at his wrists. "I mean, I've been so careful, honestly I have, but look what happened—I still ended up in the hospital. Can you imagine what might have happened if I hadn't been paying attention to every meal and every step I take?"

Tears filled her eyes as her voice drifted off, and he

reached up to dab the moisture from her lashes. "You're doing a great job," he reassured her. "You were just working too hard, and even that was for the baby."

Her lips continued to tremble, so he covered them with his own, hoping to kiss away any lingering doubts she might have about her abilities as a mother. He kept them light and comforting, sipping at the sweet nectar of her mouth rather than devouring her the way his libido urged.

When he pulled back, the uncertainty had fled her face, replaced by a simmering passion that mirrored his own.

"Have you felt the baby move yet?" he asked, not surprised when his voice came out rough and ragged.

She nodded, and the gesture sent a jolt of arousal straight to his groin.

"Will you let me know the next time it happens? I'd really like to be there, feel it for myself."

"Of course," she all but whispered.

It was enough. Now that he'd gotten the answers to his questions, they could move on to more pleasurable pursuits.

Shooting her a wicked grin, he rose to his feet, hooked her under the arms and lifted her farther back on the bed. He stretched out above her, admiring the view and thinking of all the things he wanted to do with her. They might not get through the entire list tonight, but they had time.

With luck, they would have a lot of time together.

He ran his fingers through her hair, spread in a

brown and blond halo around her head. "Have I told you lately how beautiful you are?"

Her lips turned up at the corners. "Not that I recall."

"How remiss of me," he murmured, kissing the slope of her shoulder.

He slipped his index finger under the strap of her bra and slowly drew it down her arm. Then he repeated the process on the other side.

"You are, you know. Beautiful."

She arched her back a little as he reached beneath her and released the set of hooks at her spine. The filigreed cups came loose from her voluptuous flesh and he removed the garment altogether, tossing it over the edge of the bed.

"I thought so the very first time I saw you. You were on stage with all those other dancers. Attractive women, every last one, but still you stood out."

She inhaled sharply as his fingers and then his tongue found a nipple and began to play.

"I saw you, too," she rasped. "Every once in a while, through a break in the lights, I would look out and there you were."

Her nails raked his biceps, her breaths coming in pants as he took turns licking and teasing the tender peaks of her breasts. He remembered what she'd said about their sensitivity and was careful to use just the right amount of pressure.

He slid his hands down, over her distended belly to her hips, catching the lace of her panties with his thumbs. She moved for him, helping him to get them down her legs and over her dainty feet with their rose-tipped toes.

"It's your turn to undress," she told him, when he returned to nibbling her lips. Her bare knee rubbed against his jeans.

"Mmm. Let me just take care of that. You will be here when I get back, won't you?" He shot her an errant grin, knowing full well he had her right where he wanted her.

"I'll try not to run off," she returned with a grin of her own.

While he moved off the bed, kicking away his shoes and socks and shrugging out of his pants, Misty wormed her way higher on the mattress. She fluffed the pillows at her back, reclining like an Egyptian princess awaiting the dutiful attentions of her myriad servants. If he'd had a bunch of grapes, he would have been more than happy to feed them to her one by one as he worshipped her ripe, luscious body.

But he didn't have any grapes, so he would have to simply worship.

Naked now, he crawled toward her, like a great cat stalking its prey. He didn't need a mirror to tell him his eyes burned with longing. He could feel it pulsating through every cell of his being, heating his blood, raising his temperature, sending pulses of desire to his already throbbing erection.

Kneeling in front of her, he pulled her up by her wrists. He stared at her for several long seconds, taking in her heart-shaped face, the glow of her emerald-green eyes and her velvet smooth lips, swollen from his kisses.

Wrapping one hand around her neck, beneath the curtain of her hair, he kissed her again. Devoured her mouth, suckled her tongue. He could kiss her forever, he thought, and never grow tired of her feel, her taste, her scent.

His lips still locked with hers, he shifted his weight until he was lying flat on the mattress, Misty hovering above him. Her stomach nestled against his, her breasts brushing his chest. She straddled his hips, coming close enough for her feminine heat to seep into his skin.

"It's been too long," he said, drawing her closer, urging her to take him inside before he exploded.

"I know."

Reaching between their bodies, she caressed him, making the breath hiss through his teeth and his hips hitch off the bed, straining for more of her magical touch. And then she slid down, taking him to the hilt. She fit him like a glove and felt like heaven, surrounding him with her warm wetness.

Four months since he'd last tasted her sweet mouth, cupped her full, bountiful breasts, had her tight sheath clasped around him.

How had he ever survived that long without her?

How had he ever thought another woman could take her place, or adequately fulfill his needs in between trips to Las Vegas?

And it wasn't just the sex. His head arched into

the pillows and his mouth opened on a gasp as she rose up, then dropped back down, sending ripples of ecstasy coursing through his nervous system.

When he could breathe again—albeit raggedly— he realized his last thought before she'd sent his brain spinning was still true. The sex was great— fabulous, amazing, earth-shattering—no doubt about it. But there was more to this attraction than that.

He'd asked her to marry him back at her apartment because he thought it was the right thing to do for her and for the baby. But now…now he actually wanted it for himself, too.

Being saddled with Misty for the rest of his life wasn't the worst thing he could imagine. And having her in his bed each night would be the icing on the cake.

Bracing her hands on his chest, she increased her pace, driving all rational thought from his mind. He squeezed her hips, helping her to rise and fall, rise and fall. Faster, stronger. Her inner muscles clenched around him and he gritted his teeth to keep from flying apart too soon.

"Cullen," she moaned, tossing her head back so that her hair fell in glossy multicolored waves over her naked shoulders and biting her bottom lip so hard, it turned white.

"Misty," he returned with equal emotion.

She cried out again, a high-pitched sound that re-verberated into his skin, his bones, his very soul. She shuddered above him, her nails curling like claws into his pectoral muscles as she came, and he followed her. Followed her into bliss…into their future.

When she started to collapse, he caught her and rolled them to their sides to accommodate her rounded belly.

"Well," she said, tiny beads of perspiration dotting her blushing cheeks and brow, "that was certainly an impressive way to welcome me to your home."

He chuckled, hugging her tighter and tucking strands of damp hair behind her ear with its sparkling blue-and-green stones dangling from the lobe.

"That wasn't welcome-to-my-home sex," he told her. "That was this-is-just-one-of-the-many-perks-you-can-expect-by-marrying-me sex."

He felt her stiffen in his arms even before he met her shimmering gaze, but didn't give her time to reply. "Marry me, Misty. Say yes."

Six

The lovely warmth of afterglow coursing through Misty's veins cooled at his words.

If only he knew how much she wanted to say yes.

Like most little girls, she'd spent much of her childhood and adolescence imagining her own personal happily ever after. Meeting her Prince Charming, having him sweep her up onto his white steed and carrying her off to a castle far, far away where they would live and love forever, just like a fairy tale.

But the older she'd gotten, the more she'd come to realize how much of a fantasy those daydreams had been. Men were only human, it seemed. There were very few princes in her kingdom, and many of them had more in common with the ogres who lived under the castle's drawbridge.

Cullen was definitely one of the better ones, more princely than most, but it didn't take Merlin to figure out how mismatched they were. She just wasn't the right princess for him.

Her lungs emptied on a resigned sigh as she traced patterns on his bare chest, avoiding his intense gaze. "Cullen, I told you before, I can't marry you."

Instead of arguing with her, as she'd expected, he merely shrugged one broad bronzed shoulder and said, "You can't blame a guy for trying."

She could, but she wouldn't. The fact was, even though she couldn't accept, she found his offer— *offers*—extremely flattering. And it only made her respect him more for wanting to give his child a real family and his very influential last name.

"Just…don't ask me again, okay?" she asked softly. It was too painful to be reminded of what she couldn't have, and she knew it was only going to get harder to turn him down.

"Sorry," he replied glibly, turning his body until he hovered above her and braced his weight on his strong muscled arms. "I can't make any promises."

And then he was kissing her, making her forget all her reasons for saying no.

The next morning Misty's pulse was racing and she was sweating as though she'd been sitting in a sauna for the past two hours. Her stomach lurched, and if she didn't know better, she would say she was suffering from morning sickness all over again.

This was terrible. Horrible. Pure torture. How could Cullen ask her to marry him one minute, then turn around and treat her this shabbily the next?

Meeting his parents. My God, what was he thinking?

When he popped his head in the bedroom door, she had the sudden urge to lob something at his head. Unfortunately, the only objects within reach were a drawer full of lacy undergarments. And he would probably like it if she tossed one of those at his face.

"You about ready?" he asked.

She glanced down at herself, standing in the middle of his bedroom wearing nothing but a pink bra and panties.

"Do I *look* ready?" she snapped, then felt immediately contrite. It wasn't his fault she was a nervous wreck. Although it *was* his fault she had to meet his parents.

The pregnant mistress being brought home to meet Mom and Dad. It was enough to cause heart palpitations.

Tears filled her eyes, but she turned away quickly before he noticed. She wanted to believe she was simply overly emotional because of the pregnancy, but knew it was more than that.

She was thoroughly terrified about what the next few hours would bring. Fires, floods, pestilence… The list went on and on in her head.

"Hey."

His soft low voice reached her from behind her left ear, and his hands sliding over her shoulders and down the length of her arms. Goosebumps broke out along the bare flesh.

"What's wrong?"

She gave a short bark of laugher. What *wasn't* wrong?

"I don't want to do this," she told him truthfully. "Your parents are going to hate me. They'll blame me for corrupting you, and accuse me of trying to trap you by getting pregnant, and I don't know what to wear to my own persecution." Her tirade ended on a high note, panic seeping into the words.

Cullen chuckled, rubbing her upper arms comfortingly. "Sweetheart, you're worrying for nothing. My folks are dying to meet you, and they are *not* going to treat you badly. I wouldn't allow it, even if they tried."

His reassurances were helping. Not putting an end to her fears altogether, but lightening the pressure around her lungs and diaphragm.

"Now, far be it from me to tell a woman what to wear, but as much as I'm personally enjoying your outfit, you might want to put on a few more clothes before Mom and Dad get here."

She gave a small squeak when she realized she was still in her underwear, jerking away from him and racing to the closet.

Of course, not a single thing she'd brought with

her seemed appropriate for meeting her lover's parents. At the moment, she doubted a nun's habit would have looked demure enough.

"I can't believe I let you pack for me," she ranted, her stress level rising once again. "All you brought is sexy lingerie. I can't meet your mother and father in sexy lingerie. What were you thinking?"

"I was thinking you look hot no matter what you're wearing."

He crossed the room, moving in front of her to sort through the closet's offerings. "Here, this isn't sexy lingerie."

She studied the skirt and top he was holding. It wasn't exactly demure, but it wasn't awful. A seashell pink skirt with a flounce at the bottom that would almost reach her knees, and a floral blouse with a plunging V-neckline and loose ruffled material at the shoulders in place of sleeves.

The front was a little low, but maybe she could pull it closed with a safety pin. And the pink, wine and brown floral pattern would go a long way toward camouflaging her expanding middle.

"All right," she said, taking a deep breath as she reached for the hanger.

"It even matches your bra and panties," Cullen announced proudly. "See, I'm not so bad at packing for you, after all."

Making a noncommittal sound at the back of her throat, she struggled into the skirt, fitting it around the bulk of her belly and straightening the seams.

Then she pulled the top over her head and hurried to the bathroom to check her reflection in the mirror.

She didn't look like a Mensa member, but she didn't look like the stereotypical ex-showgirl either. It would do.

Thankfully, she'd talked Cullen through the packing of her shoes and accessories, so she had chocolate-brown mules for her feet and gold hoops for her ears.

The doorbell rang just as she was arranging the earrings next to the diamond studs she rarely removed from her second holes. She jumped at the noise and began to panic all over again.

"That will be them," Cullen said, stepping into the bathroom with her.

He smiled encouragingly and pressed his lips to her cheek. "You look great. Take a deep breath and relax, then come down when you're ready, okay?"

She swallowed hard, taking that deep breath he had suggested. The chime sounded again as his footsteps moved out of the room and down the stairs.

Her stomach rolled as if she were riding the Tilt-A-Whirl at the state fair, but she forced her fingers to put the finishing touches on her loose hair and stroke on one last coat of lipstick.

She could do this, she told herself. All she had to do was put one foot in front of the other and make her way downstairs…straight into the lion's den.

Despite his claims that Misty had nothing to worry about, Cullen had to admit he, too, was nervous about this meeting.

Soon after discovering that Misty was pregnant, he'd phoned both of his parents from the hospital to let them know they were going to be grandparents. Since Daniel and Amanda Elliott had divorced long ago, it had taken two separate calls and two separate confessions about his four-year-long affair with Misty.

His father had gotten himself into a similar situation at the age of eighteen and had been forced to marry his mother by his old-fashioned, overbearing father—Cullen's grandfather, Patrick Elliott. So in many ways, Cullen had expected a lecture.

He should have been more careful; he never should have gotten involved with a showgirl to begin with; she was likely nothing more than a manipulative gold-digger…. But since the horse was out of the barn, so to speak, it was time for Cullen to step up and do the responsible thing.

He'd expected to hear all of that and more from his father. Instead, Daniel had been sympathetic and understanding of the situation his son found himself in. He'd offered only one piece of advice: Do what you feel is right.

His father hadn't spoken the words, but his meaning was clear: He didn't want Cullen making the same mistakes he had, letting himself be forced or guilted into marriage simply because a child was involved.

Cullen got the feeling that if he married Misty, his father would be accepting of his decision. And if he decided to be a long-distance father, that would be okay, too.

The call to his mother had been very different in tone, but essentially the same. Amanda Elliott may have been a high-priced Manhattan attorney, but her voice had grown thick and waterlogged the minute she heard she was going to be a grandmother. She'd begged him to bring Misty to New York as soon as she was feeling well enough. Or, if that wasn't convenient, Amanda herself would fly to Las Vegas so they could meet.

The topic of marriage had never come up. Either because his mother expected him to do the right thing, or because it simply didn't matter to her. Only the impending grandchild mattered.

Then last night, after he and Misty had arrived at his town house, he'd phoned them each again while Misty was unpacking her things and invited them over to meet their future daughter-in-law. He hadn't said anything about his proposal or the fact that Misty had turned him down—twice.

After taking the steps two at a time, he crossed the small foyer to the front door and yanked it open before the bell could peal again. The sound was beginning to grate on his nerves, and he could only imagine the effect it was having on Misty.

His mother and father stood on the other side of the ornately carved door. It wasn't very often that he saw them together, and he was struck once again by what a handsome couple they made.

He'd come to terms with their divorce years ago, but the little boy in him still wished they could have made things work. That he and Bryan hadn't had to go through the emotional upheaval of their split.

He didn't want that for his child. If Misty ever agreed to marry him, he would move heaven and earth to make sure they stayed together.

"Hey, Mom. Dad." He stepped back and waved them inside.

"Oh, Cullen," his mother cried, throwing her arms around his neck and hugging him tight. "I'm so happy for you."

When she let go, he noticed the hint of moisture in her brown eyes. "I know all of this came as a surprise, but you're going to make a wonderful father."

"Thanks, Mom."

Covering her heart with her hand, she went on as though he hadn't even spoken. "And *I'll* finally get to be a grandmother."

Cullen turned to face his father. "Dad."

Daniel Elliott put his hand out to shake, then pulled Cullen close and patted his back in a supportive, fatherly gesture.

For a minute, Cullen thought he might tear up himself, but cleared his throat and was relieved when the sensation passed.

"So where is this young woman we're supposed to meet? The one who's carrying our grandchild." There was no censure in his tone, only curiosity.

"She's upstairs. She had a bit of trouble deciding what to wear."

"I know the feeling," his mother replied with a smile.

"Look," he told them, stepping closer and lowering his voice. "Misty is really nervous about meeting the two of you, so try not to make her any more uncomfortable than she already is. No nosy questions or inappropriate comments about her former choice of profession, okay?"

A flash of hurt crossed his mother's face, and he felt immediately contrite.

"We wouldn't dream of it, dear."

He released a pent-up breath, rubbing his damp palms on the legs of his chinos. "I know. I just…I don't want her getting stressed out and landing in the hospital again."

His dad clapped him on the back and shot him a teasing grin. "Stop worrying, son. Your mother and I will be on our best behavior."

While they waited for Misty to make an appearance, Amanda said, "Did you hear about your cousin Scarlet and John Harlan?"

Cullen's brows knit. "No, what about them?"

"They're engaged to be married," Daniel supplied.

"Isn't that wonderful?" Amanda asked.

"Yeah." That certainly explained their odd behavior at Une Nuit the last time he'd seen them, Cullen thought. "I'll have to be sure to give them both a call to congratulate them." Not to mention give his friend a rough time for keeping him in the dark.

Before Cullen could say more, he heard a sound at the top of the stairs and spun around to see Misty standing on the second-story landing. She looked beautiful and his heart swelled with pride.

This was the woman he planned to marry. The mother of his child. The only woman he'd ever intentionally introduced to his parents.

And even though he was slightly anxious about how this morning's gathering would go, he wasn't uneasy about Misty or embarrassed by her in any way.

He hoped his family wouldn't be, either.

"Misty, sweetheart. Come on down here and meet my parents."

Her heart was racing, her palms sweating and for a second, dizziness washed over her so that she had to clutch the mahogany railing even tighter in her already white fingers.

It didn't help that Cullen had called her sweetheart. She couldn't remember him uttering the endearment in the four years they'd been sleeping together, and now he was using it in front of his mother and father.

As she moved slowly down the steps, she took in the couple standing beside Cullen.

Only about an inch shorter than his son, Daniel Elliott was dressed in a dapper dark blue suit, the jacket left unbuttoned for a more casual look. His jet black hair and blue eyes were so much like Cullen's, it was obvious they were related, though it was hard to believe Daniel was old enough to be Cullen's father. She knew he had to be in his late forties, but he could easily have passed for five or ten years younger.

Amanda Elliott had dark brown hair that fell to her chin, and equally brown eyes. She was a few inches shorter than both her ex-husband and son, with a curvaceous figure tucked into her stylish red skirt and matching jacket.

At the moment, all three Elliotts were standing at the base of the stairs, watching her descent with what appeared to be a mixture of eagerness and trepidation.

She didn't blame them. If it weren't for Cullen flashing her that encouraging smile, she'd have run back upstairs and locked herself in the bathroom long before now.

As soon as she came within reach, Cullen took her hand and pulled her close to his side. She went willingly, needing both his physical and emotional support. He kept his fingers wrapped around hers and slipped his other arm around her waist, so that his palm rested on the curve of her pregnant belly.

"Mom, Dad," he said proudly, "this is Misty Vale."

A beat of complete, taut silence passed, and then his mother threw up her arms and gave Misty an enthusiastic hug. "Welcome to the family," she singsonged. "And, oh, look at you!"

Leaning back, she curved both hands over Misty's protruding stomach, circling the firm, round mass. Misty stiffened, surprised by the woman's forwardness. But then she relaxed, reminding herself that this was Cullen's mother…her child's grandmother.

"Misty." Cullen's father reached around his ex-wife's exuberant form to shake her hand. "Like Amanda said, welcome to the family."

Her chest swelled at their kindness, and for a minute, she felt like an Elliott. Like Cullen's true fiancée rather than his pregnant mistress.

She cleared her throat, praying her vocal chords would work. "Thank you, but I'm not really family. I'm just—"

Daniel cut her off before she had a chance to grope for the appropriate description. "You're carrying my son's child, the next generation of Elliotts. That makes you family."

Tears burned her eyes and her lungs refused to take in air. She turned her gaze to Cullen, squeezing his hand in a death grip, desperate to be rescued before she collapsed into a grateful, sobbing mess in front of his parents.

"Why don't we go into the kitchen," he said, flexing his fingers around hers reassuringly. "Misty and I haven't had breakfast yet. You're welcome to join us, or I can get you a cup of coffee while we talk."

Seven

While they chatted, Cullen made omelets. Misty told him she wasn't hungry—in truth, she still felt too nervous to eat—but he insisted. She was eating for two now, he took great joy in pointing out, and then he proceeded to fill her beaten egg mixture with every possible fresh vegetable.

She had to admit, it was delicious. The first few bites had been forced to keep from hurting his feelings, but now she realized just how famished she'd actually been, and ate with relish.

Having already eaten before their arrival, Daniel and Amanda passed on the offer of breakfast, settling for cups of coffee instead.

Misty knew they were divorced, and from what

Cullen had told her about the split, she understood things hadn't always been amicable. But no one would know it by the way they were acting this morning.

Daniel had pulled out Amanda's stool for her before taking a seat at the counter beside her. And when Cullen had handed them mugs of steaming black coffee, Daniel had automatically flavored his ex-wife's with cream and sugar.

And Amanda had let him. She'd acted as though such behavior was completely normal.

Hmm. Misty wouldn't say anything to Cullen in case she was wrong, but it looked to her like a few sparks might be flaring to life again between them.

"It's not that I'm not delighted for you," Cullen's father said in a reserved tone, "but you know how your grandfather is. He's sure to have something to say about this, and it probably won't be nice."

Misty chewed carefully, watching the three Elliotts exchange knowing glances.

"Well, you know how I feel about that," Amanda replied, fingers wrapped tightly around her ceramic cup. "I'd tell the old coot to go to hell. How you live your life is nobody's business but your own. My own life certainly would have turned out a lot differently if Patrick Elliott hadn't been such an overbearing tyrant."

Though the words were caustic, Amanda's voice held no hostility. She seemed to be merely stating facts and telling her son not to let his grandfather's opinion influence his actions in any way.

Misty didn't know what to think. She'd been expecting Cullen's parents to treat her with derision, but they hadn't. And now they were telling her that his grandfather likely would. It was enough to send Cullen's light-as-air omelet sinking like a stone in her stomach.

"I can't help what Granddad thinks," Cullen told his parents, his mouth turned down in a hint of a frown. "If I get the chance, I'll drive out to the Tides and talk with him. Maybe he'll handle the situation better if he hears it directly from me."

Daniel nodded solemnly. Amanda sipped at her coffee and refrained from comment.

Setting her fork down, Misty pushed her plate away and folded her hands in her lap, appetite suddenly gone. The entire scene made her uncomfortable. They were discussing her as if she wasn't even in the room.

She understood that her unexpected pregnancy impacted the entire Elliott family, but didn't want to be a bone of contention between anyone. Especially if it meant that Cullen's relationship with his father or grandfather would be negatively affected…or Daniel's relationship with *his* father.

"You don't have to do that," she told Cullen. "I don't want to cause trouble with anyone in your family. I can just as easily go back to Henderson and—"

"No." His response was sharp and fast. "You're staying here. And you're not causing trouble…you're having my baby. Granddad can accept that or not. The choice is his, but it doesn't affect us."

"Cullen…" she tried again.

"Misty…" he said with a smile, then swooped in for a quick, hard kiss. "No. Let it go."

She wasn't sure how to respond to that, at least not without starting a heated argument in front of his parents.

Daniel checked his watch, then cleared his throat to break the uncomfortable silence as he pushed back his stool. "I'd better get going. *Snap* won't run itself, you know. Although I'll understand if you don't come in for a couple of days," he added with a pointed glance at his son.

"Oh, my goodness, look at the time." Amanda jumped up, too, tugging at the hem of her tailored jacket. "Daniel isn't the only one who needs to get a move on. I've got to meet a client. Misty, it was lovely to meet you. I'm looking forward to spending even more time with you while you're in town."

She rounded the counter to give her son a peck on the cheek, then wrapped Misty in a smothering hug. "You two have fun today, and take care of my grandbaby."

Misty jumped as Amanda's manicured hand once again rubbed her belly, but managed a nod. In fact, Amanda's unconditional acceptance of her choked her up.

Amanda left the kitchen with Daniel on her heels.

"I'll walk you out," Cullen said. He ran a hand absently across Misty's arm before following his parents. "You stay here and finish your omelet."

Misty could see the three of them clearly from

her perch in the kitchen, and noticed that when Amanda stopped to retrieve her purse, Daniel laid a hand on her shoulder. There was definitely something going on between them, she decided. And in a way, it gave her hope.

Knowing that Daniel and Amanda could be forced to marry because of an unexpected pregnancy and still care for each other all these years later made her think she and Cullen might have a chance, too.

If she agreed to marry him, would they be doomed for failure…or might they eventually grow to love each other?

Cullen stood inside the open door, waving goodbye to his mother. His father stood on the front stoop a moment longer, and as soon as Amanda was out of sight, turned back to face him.

"If you do speak with your grandfather, let me know what he says. I agree that you shouldn't let his rigid and sometimes outdated views control your life, but he could make things difficult for both you and Misty. I just wanted to warn you of that."

The shadows in his dad's eyes told him better than words how much Daniel regretted parts of his own past. Cullen didn't want to make the same mistakes, but so far, it seemed he was following pretty darn closely in his father's footsteps.

"Thanks, Dad. I know Granddad won't be too happy when he hears I got a former showgirl pregnant, but hopefully in time he'll come around."

"Yeah, hopefully. In time," Daniel agreed with a twist to his lips. "Look, son, it's none of my business, but have you considered doing the right thing by her? Marrying her, I mean."

"I asked," Cullen admitted. "She turned me down."

His father's eyes widened, but to his credit, he kept his mouth shut.

"Don't worry," Cullen added, "I'm working on it. And I fully intend to change her mind before long."

After a moment, Daniel nodded. "I'm sure you will."

Seconds ticked by while Daniel remained just outside the front door, not meeting Cullen's gaze, but not walking away, either. Clearing his throat, he said, "There's something else I've been meaning to tell you. My marriage to Sharon is finally over."

Cullen watched the tension flash across his father's face, disappearing with his announcement. His divorce from his second wife had been long and drawn-out, with Sharon doing her best to take Daniel for everything he was worth.

Laying a hand on his father's arm, he gave a quick, supportive squeeze. "I'm glad, Dad."

Daniel nodded and they said their goodbyes before Cullen headed back to the kitchen. Misty hadn't eaten any more of her omelet, he noted, but she'd finished off the glass of milk he'd poured for her.

Good. He knew she was taking prenatal vitamins, but he intended to make sure she ate well while she was here, too.

"So…what did you think of my mom and dad?" he asked, helping her hop down from the stool. He held her a few seconds longer than was necessary, enjoying the feel of her bare arms under his hands and her belly bumping into his.

"They were very nice. Wonderful, really." She chewed thoughtfully on her lower lip. "I didn't expect them to be so accepting of me or our situation."

"I told you they would be. My mother is through the roof at the prospect of being a grandmother." He shot her a wide grin. "In case you couldn't tell."

She chuckled and threw her arms around his neck. "I noticed. I've never had someone spend so much time feeling my belly."

"Oh, yeah?" He slipped his hand between them and did just that.

"Well, except for you, of course. I don't think you stopped touching my stomach all night, even in your sleep."

"Get used to it," he told her. "I have a lot of lost moments to make up for, and I plan to spend as much time as possible caressing your adorable pregnant body."

His palm slid around her waist, to the small of her back, then the curve of her buttocks. A moan rumbled in her throat as her head fell back and he covered the pulse there with his lips.

"So what do you say?" he murmured against her warm skin. "Ready to marry me yet?"

He felt her muscles tighten for a second, then relax.

"Not yet," she answered just before turning her face to his for a slow, lazy kiss.

Maybe she was coming around, he thought as her fingers danced down his arms and her tongue began to do wild, sexy things inside his mouth.

Because *not yet* didn't necessarily mean *no*.

They made love right there in the kitchen, with Cullen being as careful with her as he would be with a delicate piece of china.

Then, after rearranging their clothes, Cullen offered to show her the city. He'd taken the day off, anyway, and she'd never been to New York before.

He wouldn't let her overexert herself, so they took a cab to Central Park, where they spent hours of a sunny May afternoon strolling hand-in-hand, admiring the trees and fountains and children playing.

He showed her the Statue of Liberty, the Empire State Building, Radio City Music Hall and gave her a leisurely tour of the Elliott Publication Holdings building on Park Avenue, between Fiftieth and Fifty-first Streets.

The lobby alone took up two stories, with tall windows, granite floors and so many live trees and plants that it looked like a conservatory.

Cullen stopped at one of the large granite security stations to check her in and get her a guest pass. It probably wasn't necessary, he told her, but this way she wouldn't cause questions or concern if they happened to split up.

At the bank of elevators, he scanned his own identification card and they headed upstairs.

Mailing and shipping for the entire building took up the third floor, the cafeteria the fourth, and the gym was on the fifth. She knew for a fact Cullen spent a good amount of time using the weights and machines there; she felt the proof of that beneath her fingertips every time they made love.

They skipped levels six through eighteen and twenty through twenty-four, which held various meeting rooms, boardrooms and magazine offices, heading straight for *Snap* on nineteen.

As the elevator whisked them silently upward, he explained which magazines were housed on which floors and what the publications entailed in a way he hadn't before. She was familiar with EPH, of course—soon after they'd begun their affair, she'd made a point of studying as much as she could about the Elliott empire without letting him know—but he seemed more in his element now, more willing to take the time to share details.

The fifteenth floor, he told her, was dedicated to *HomeStyle* magazine, known for its focus on fashion for the home; seventeen housed *Charisma*—fashion for the body; and *Snap* was sandwiched between their showbiz publication, *The Buzz,* on eighteen and *Pulse* for the news on twenty.

It was enough to make her head spin, but she listened intently and nodded in all the right places because Cullen's job and his family's business really did fascinate her.

The elevator doors swished open and Cullen led her off the car. With her hand in his, she stopped in her tracks and stared.

"Oh, Cullen, it's beautiful."

He threw her a pleased smile. "We like it."

The entire floor was decorated in black and white and screamed Old Hollywood. Small framed photographs of Marilyn Monroe and James Cagney adorned the walls, along with much larger prints of some of *Snap*'s most famous covers.

It made her think of old black-and-white gangster films and starlets with breathless voices and hourglass figures today's women could only dream of—which she supposed was the point.

Over the years, he'd described parts of his work environment, but she'd never imagined this. And now that she'd seen it, she knew she would never be able to picture him anywhere else. It suited him.

He introduced her to *Snap*'s petite brunette receptionist before she buzzed them through the glass doors that divided the reception area from the rest of the floor. Voices, ringing phones and the sounds of a bustling business filled the air as they moved between cubicles toward his office.

Misty was impressed by how many of EPH's employees—Cullen's coworkers—greeted him with a smile and wave, and seemed more than willing to accept her as one of Cullen's close personal friends.

She wasn't sure if they saw her as simply that—a friend—or assumed more was going on between them. They didn't ask and Cullen didn't tell. But either way, they were warm and pleasant, and made her feel more than welcome.

When they reached his office, he opened the door stamped *Cullen Elliott, Director of Sales* and ushered her inside.

"Very nice," she told him, noticing that the room's vintage décor matched the rest of the floor's.

"Thanks." He let go of her hand and rounded his desk. "Let me just check a couple of things, then we can get going."

"Take your time."

She wandered around the room, studying some of the framed magazine covers on the wall, his business degree and personal pictures.

Near his desk, she chanced a glance over his shoulder as he sifted through phone messages and memos. It took her a moment to realize he'd stopped moving and was now looking directly at her.

"Sorry." Her cheeks heated and she took a step back, ready to return to her perusal of his photo gallery.

"Don't be silly." He grabbed her hand and pulled her onto his lap. "I was just thinking how beautiful you are, and how I wish I never had to come into work again so I could stay home twenty-four hours and worship you like the goddess you are."

"Cullen…" Her laugh sounded brittle as she slapped at his chest.

"What's the matter?" he asked with a chuckle of his own. "You don't think I could do it?"

"Oh, I have no doubt you could do it, but—"

"Kiss me."

"What?"

"Kiss me. Give me something to fantasize about when I'm locked in this dark, dreary office, working my fingers to the bone."

She hardly thought of his office as *dreary,* even with a copious amount of black mixed with the white. But she leaned in and kissed him all the same, enjoying the warmth of his lips, his hands at her back.

"Knock, knock."

Misty jumped at the unexpected female voice, quickly breaking away from Cullen's embrace and getting to her feet. She turned her attention to the tall, attractive blonde standing just inside the room, her hand still on the doorknob.

"Hey, Bridge," Cullen said, though he sounded less than pleased by the interruption.

"Sorry, didn't mean to intrude, but I heard you two were in the building and just had to come up and meet Misty for myself."

She moved forward, holding her hand out for Misty's. Misty took it and let the woman shake her arm exuberantly.

"Misty, this is my cousin Bridget. She's the photo editor for *Charisma* down on seventeen. Bridget, this is Misty Vale."

"It's nice to meet you," Misty said reflexively.

"It's *really* nice to meet you," Bridget returned, then backed up a few steps and plopped down in one of the guest chairs positioned in front of Cullen's desk.

She was wearing a tight black skirt and black heels. Her blue blouse was sheer, with draping medieval sleeves and a low neckline that did a great job of showcasing her cleavage. The girl had fashion sense, that was for sure, and Misty found herself liking Cullen's cousin immediately. She was even thinking of asking where she'd gotten her top.

"I have to tell you, Misty, you're the hottest topic to hit the Elliott grapevine in ages. Granddad's furious. 'No grandson of mine is going to marry a stripper,'" she mimicked in a low, crusty tone.

Bridget made a face, rolling her eyes. "Please. If you ask me, the Elliotts could use some fresh blood in the old family tree. And it doesn't get any fresher than a Las Vegas showgirl," she added with a grin.

Misty felt the blood drain from her face and held a hand out toward the desk in case she started to sway.

"Bridge…" Cullen muttered in warning, apparently noticing her distress.

"Uncle Daniel and Aunt Amanda are over the moon, though. They're so excited about Cullen getting married and giving them a grandchild, they're just about floating. I wouldn't be surprised if Aunt Amanda is already planning the wedding."

"Bridge…"

"And you absolutely *must* tell me how the two of you met and got together. I have yet to hear the real story. All I've gotten are snippets, and I think most of them are merely conjecture. I'd much rather get it from the horses' mouths, if you—"

"*Bridget!*"

Bridget blinked her blue eyes, her mouth left open. "Yes?"

"Shut. Up."

Eight

Bridget blinked again, the shock on her face showing she was completely unaware of why Cullen was yelling at her. He took a deep breath and unclenched his teeth, trying to shake off the annoyance his cousin's little diatribe had created.

"I didn't mean to snap," he told her calmly, "but I think you're making Misty uneasy."

Bridget glanced at Misty, her eyes going wide in comprehension. She leapt out of her chair and raced to give her an apologetic hug. "Oh, my gosh, I'm so sorry, I had no idea."

When she returned to her seat, she dragged Misty along, urging her into the chair beside her. "I didn't mean to offend you or make you uncomfortable. I'm just so excited about having you in the family, my mouth got away from me."

"As usual," Cullen mumbled, then shot his cousin a wink and a grin when she scowled at him.

"It's all right," Misty said, smoothing a hand over her stomach, then clutching the arms of her chair until her fingers whitened.

"No, it's not. I shouldn't have come on so strong. You've only been in town for one day. You probably haven't even unpacked, and here I am putting you on the spot about the rest of your life."

She shook her head, sending her shoulder-length hair into motion before reaching over to clasp one of Misty's hands. "Forgive me. I'd like for us to be friends, and I don't want you to think that I'm going to be the nosy or presumptuous kind."

Cullen watched the two women exchange a look. As soon as Misty began to smile, Bridget did, too. His heart, which had stopped beating for the barest space of a second, picked up again and he released a silent sigh of relief.

He hoped Misty and his cousin could be friends. The more Elliotts who welcomed Misty with open arms and treated her like family right off the bat, the better his chances of convincing her to marry him…convincing her to stay.

"So what do you say I give you a call one of these days and we can go out to lunch, maybe do a little shopping?"

Misty's lips tipped up in pleasure. "I'd like that."

"Great. I'd better get back to work," Bridget said, patting Misty's knee and rising to her feet. "And leave you two to get back to whatever you were doing."

She flashed Cullen a teasing grin, wiggling her fingers as she waved goodbye. Cullen couldn't help but grin himself as the door closed behind her.

"In case you missed it," he deadpanned, "that was my cousin, Bridget."

Misty gave a breathless laugh. "So I gathered. She's very…"

"Yeah, she is. But she's a terrific girl. If she calls to ask you out to lunch or shopping, you should take her up on it. I really think you two will hit it off."

Pushing back his rolling leather chair, he stood and moved in front of Misty and took her hands. She offered them willingly, and he pulled her up until her long, lithe body rested all along the length of his own. He leaned back against the edge of the desk, taking her with him.

"Now, where were we?" he asked, looking deeply into her emerald-green eyes.

"You were checking your messages," she answered almost too innocently.

The corners of his mouth stretched in a grin. "That's not how I remember it. As I recall, you were sitting on my lap and I was wondering if I could talk you into a little interoffice hanky-panky."

"Why, Mr. Elliott," she said, feigning offense, "that could be construed as sexual harassment."

"Only if you work for me, which you don't.

And only if you aren't interested, which I'm pretty sure you are."

She made a purring sound of agreement, her fingers toying with the hair at the nape of his neck. That action alone sent shivers of desire sliding in a domino effect down the line of his vertebrae.

He was just leaning in to kiss her, hoping for a lot more, when the phone rang.

"Son of a…" He scowled at the offending object, silently wishing it to Hades.

"Aren't you going to answer it?"

Careful not to dump her on the floor, Cullen got up and set Misty on her feet. "Hell, no. Let it go to voice mail. I'll deal with it tomorrow."

Taking her hand, he straightened a couple of things on his desk, then led her to the door. "Let's get out of here before something—or some*one*—else interrupts us."

On the way to his town house on the Upper West Side, Cullen told the cab driver to take the long way, cruising down Broadway so Misty could *ooh* and *ahh* over the brightly lit marquees.

She'd never seen a Broadway play before, and he promised to escort her to any shows she wanted, any time she wanted. Of course, there were entirely too many to choose from, and in order to attend more than one or two, she would have to stay in Manhattan with him…and she wasn't at all sure that was how things would work out.

They arrived home late in the afternoon, and though she had expected him to pick up where they had left off in his office, when they reached the bedroom, he instead insisted she lie down to rest. She was having too much fun and didn't want to sleep, but he promised to take her out to dinner if she did— to his brother's restaurant, Une Nuit, no less.

It was an offer she couldn't refuse, and as soon as her head hit the pillow, she realized she must have been exhausted after all, because she drifted immediately off to sleep.

When she opened her eyes several hours later, Cullen was seated on the edge of the bed, smiling down at her. She startled at first, then pulled herself up to sit with her back against the headboard.

"How long have you been watching me sleep?"

"Just a few minutes."

She ran her fingers through her hair, sure it was a mess, then brushed at her mouth and the corners of her eyes. "Did I drool?" she wanted to know.

He chuckled. "No. You're beautiful—and very ladylike—when you sleep."

"Thank goodness. Is it time to go to dinner?"

"We can go any time you're ready. Bryan has the family booth reserved for us, so there's no hurry."

He'd exchanged his casual clothes for a more formal pair of tailored black slacks and jacket with a white dress shirt underneath. Thankfully, she'd brought a black knit dress along that would be appropriate for dinner at his brother's upscale restaurant.

"Let me change," she said, throwing back the covers and sliding off the king-size mattress.

She thought he'd leave the room while she got ready, but he stayed where he was, watching her every move. If she hadn't spent the past four years walking nearly or fully naked around him, she might have been embarrassed.

As it was, she barely would have noticed his presence if she hadn't felt the heat of his gaze searing her skin while she stripped out of her skirt and top and slipped into black stockings and the versatile little black dress. Thankfully, the material stretched to cover the bump of her belly without needing alterations or camouflage to look decent.

Ten minutes later, she was ready to go. Cullen held her hand as they left the house and slowly walked the two short blocks to Une Nuit.

The restaurant was brimming with people when they arrived. Customers, dressed to the nines, smiled and laughed over their meals while the waitstaff bustled between tables taking orders and serving food.

Misty was immediately impressed by the ambience and popularity of Bryan's establishment. Black suede banquettes and armchairs surrounded copper-topped tables, with low red lighting illuminating the entire space. She was used to bright and glitzy, but Une Nuit was the epitome of trendy but romantic.

As soon as the maitre d' saw them, he smiled and led them through the main dining room to a private booth reserved for members of the Elliott family whenever they chose to drop by. Cullen gestured for her to take a place behind the table, then slid in next to her, thighs brushing.

She was almost too distracted by her surroundings to think about eating, but Cullen leaned close to tell her about the different appetizers and entrées; which ones he'd tried, which were his favorites, which were restaurant specialties. Everything sounded wonderful to her.

After they placed their orders, Cullen moved in tighter, putting his arm around her shoulders.

"What do you think?" he asked, tipping his head toward the center of the dining area.

"If the food is half as wonderful as the atmosphere, I'll think your brother is a genius. This place is amazing."

"Hey, you finally landed a smart one, little brother."

Misty jumped at the intrusion, but Cullen merely grinned up at the man hovering behind them over the back of the booth.

So this was Bryan she thought, as he swung around and took a seat across from them. He was tall, with the same black hair and blue eyes as his younger brother and father had. The family resemblance was so strong, even if a person hadn't known they were Elliotts, they would immediately realize the three men were related.

"Misty," Cullen said, waving an arm in his brother's direction, "meet my brother, Bryan. He's the owner of this fine establishment and an all-around pain in the ass."

"Funny," Bryan remarked, "when we were kids, that's what I used to say about you."

They were like two puppies wrestling over the same chew toy, and she couldn't help but smile.

Bryan held his hand out over the table's centerpiece, a shallow bowl of water with three floating lighted ivory candles in the shape of some stunning exotic flower.

Misty returned his quick shake.

"It's nice to meet you, Misty. Is my brother treating you okay?"

"I'm treating her just fine," Cullen answered for her. "Unlike some men, I know how to treat a lady."

"Don't let him fool you," Bryan said, flashing her an amused wink. "Everything he knows, he learned from his big brother."

Cullen scoffed, and Misty could only grin.

"So how are you two doing?" Bryan asked, turning serious, his gaze focusing mainly on Misty. "Has the family given you a warm and friendly welcome?"

She toyed with the rim of her drink glass, feeling suddenly nervous, just like she did every time the topic of Cullen's family—or being welcomed into it—came up.

"Oh, yes, they've all been very nice."

"Even Granddad?" This time, his clear blue eyes went straight to his brother.

"He'll come around," Cullen responded simply.

Bryan's attention skidded away from them to a spot far beyond their booth. "Sorry I can't stick around, but I'm being beckoned. A restaurateur's job is never done. Misty, it was great to meet you. I'm looking forward to having you as my sister-in-law."

He flashed her a smile and offered his hand again. "Enjoy your meals. Order whatever you like, it's on the house."

"That isn't necessary," Cullen told him.

"Of course, it is. Consider it my gift to you to celebrate your engagement."

He waved his arm one last time before disappearing into the heart of Une Nuit.

"Our engagement?" Misty repeated, brows arching with interest as she sipped her nonalcoholic cocktail.

Cullen cleared his throat. "I may have mentioned something along those lines when I told him we'd be dropping by."

"But we're not engaged," she pointed out.

"We would be if you'd say yes to one of my proposals."

She fought the grin that threatened to break out across her face. He sounded petulant, as though she was keeping him from something he really, really wanted. It was flattering and warmed her deep down in places only Cullen seemed capable of touching.

Still, she didn't want to joke about marriage to him or lead him to believe she would eventually accept— no matter how much she might want to.

"I'm sorry, Cullen," was all she could think to say.

For a moment, his stern expression remained, and

then his eyes lightened from a dark, stormy blue to the color of the sky in summer.

"Don't apologize," he told her. "I fully intend to wear you down. Besides, I didn't bring you here to propose to you again, or to make you feel guilty for saying no. I brought you here for dinner, and to impress you with another branch of my family tree so you would have an inkling of what awaited you if you ever did say yes. Are you adequately impressed?"

The tilt of his lips was too adorable to resist. She leaned over and pressed a kiss to his cheek.

"I'm very impressed," she said softly. "Thank you."

Their meals came then and they spent the next hour eating, talking and flirting. Cullen fed her bits of his entrée from his own fork, and she returned the favor, until things turned so hot, she was afraid they'd set the room on fire.

The sight of his lips moving as he chewed set her skin to tingling. The feel of his thigh pressed to hers heated her blood to a near boil. And from the look in Cullen's eyes, he was as aroused as she was.

"Let's get out of here," he said, snagging her hand and sliding out of the booth as soon as they'd finished the last of their desserts of crème brûlée flavored with mango and passion fruit juices.

"What about the check?"

"I hadn't planned on it, but I think I'll take Bryan up on his offer."

He stopped in the middle of the restaurant, nearly causing her to bump into his back. Spinning on his heel to face her, he drew her close and kissed her like a man stranded in the desert without food or water who had suddenly stumbled upon a bubbling oasis.

She responded, heedless of the fact that they were standing in the middle of his brother's very popular and very crowded restaurant. When he finally pulled away, diners were staring at them, but Misty couldn't find it in her to care.

"I'll pay him back later," he rasped in her ear. "For now, I just want to get you home so I can strip you down and make love to you for the rest of the night."

That sounded good to her. Heart pounding in her ears, legs the consistency of grape jelly, she nodded and uttered the only word her passion laden brain would allow. "Okay."

Nine

As much as he did not want to, Cullen returned to work the next day. Luckily, his eyes popped open a little before 6:00 a.m., before the alarm could wake Misty. Lifting her arm from his chest, he climbed carefully out of bed and began getting dressed.

Somewhere deep in his gut, he liked the idea of having her curled up under the covers every morning while he got ready to leave for the office. He liked watching her while she slept, knowing that if he climbed back in beside her, she would welcome him with open arms and use her hands and mouth to convince him to call in sick.

Stifling a groan, he tightened the knot of his tie, gave his libido the "down boy" command and forced himself to walk out of the room with only one last wishful glance at her lush sleeping form.

The morning moved at a snail's pace and he could barely concentrate on the tasks in front of him until he glanced at his watch and realized Misty would likely be out of bed by now.

He picked up the phone and punched in his own number. It rang several times before voice mail kicked in.

Dammit. Knowing Misty, she probably didn't want to answer his home phone because she knew—or rather, assumed—no one would be calling there for her.

He hung up and immediately redialed. He'd keep trying, he thought, but if she still didn't answer, a quick trip home wasn't out of the question.

"Hello?"

Her voice was tentative, nervous.

"Good morning, sexy."

"Good morning," she said, her tone still low, but sounding much more confident. "I didn't know if I should answer your phone or not, but when it kept ringing, I thought it might be important."

"For the record, you *can* answer my phone. Don't forget, Bridget might call to invite you out. If it's anyone else, you can take a message." A beat passed while he let that sink in, then he added, "And it is important. I miss you."

Silence greeted him for the space of several seconds before she murmured, "I miss you, too. This place is awfully big and quiet without you."

Damn. He thought of her in his big empty town house and went hard. He thought of her in his big empty town house, missing him, wishing he were with her, and that hardness turned to a throbbing painful ache.

"I'm coming home," he grated out through a throat gone closed with desire.

She laughed, the light tinkling sound carrying over the phone line. "No, you aren't. You have work to do."

"It can wait." He didn't think making love to her could.

"Don't be silly. You've taken enough time off to cater to me, and I'll still be here when you get home."

Cullen didn't know which warmed him more—hearing her call his place "home" or hearing her say she'd be there when he got back. A part of him knew she could pick up and fly back to Nevada at any moment. He could walk in the door one day and find her gone.

"In the meantime, I thought I'd wander around, snooping in all your cupboards and drawers," she went on. "Are you hiding any naughty secrets you don't want me to find?"

His lips curled up in a grin. "Sweetheart, for you, I'm an open book."

"Mmm," she purred in response. "Interesting concept."

"Well, if you're not going to let me come home and rock your world, then I suppose I should get back to work."

"All right. I'll see you tonight, then."

"I'll call if I'm going to be late."

"Okay."

"Hey, Misty," he said before she could hang up.

"Yes?"

"Will you marry me?"

He could almost see her eyes widen in sudden panic, the pulse in her neck pick up speed.

"Not today," she finally answered. "But thank you for asking."

Despite being rejected for what must have been the fifth or sixth time, he found himself smiling. "I guess I'll just have to ask again tomorrow."

The next day, and every day after, Cullen called home several times, just to hear Misty's voice. And while he had her on the line, he always made sure to ask her the same question. "Will you marry me?"

Each time, her answer remained unchanged, but he didn't stop trying. If anything, her refusal made him more determined. Like a medieval warrior, he would continue to storm her castle walls until they crumbled and she gave in to the inevitable.

A week or so later, Cullen made his way to the EPH gym where he was meeting his brother for a midday exercise session. He tried to work out for an hour every day, and whenever Bryan could make it, he joined in.

After changing into shorts and a sweatshirt with

the neck and arms cut out, Cullen headed for the free weights. Bryan joined him and they both began to do arm curls.

"So how are things going between you and Misty?" his brother wanted to know.

"Great," Cullen answered honestly.

Things between them were fabulous. The sex was earth-shattering, as always, and he found her near-constant company more intriguing than he could have imagined.

He was never bored with her, and that was more than he could say about any other woman he'd ever dated. If only she would accept one of his countless marriage proposals, life would be perfect.

"Has she taken you up on your offer to marry her yet?"

Cullen ignored the slight smirk on his brother's face. "No. I'm still working on it, though. She'll come around eventually."

"Are you sure you want her to?"

At Bryan's softly spoken question, Cullen's movements slowed. "What's that supposed to mean?"

"Hey…" Bryan held up his free hand, continuing reps with the other. "I'm not trying to piss you off. I'm just asking if getting married is what you really want, or if you're only asking because you got her pregnant."

If a comment like that had come out of anyone else's mouth, he'd have already driven his fist into the offender's teeth. But his brother was his best friend and confidant, and Cullen knew he meant well.

"I'm not sure," Cullen said, for the first time putting voice to his true feelings. "I want to marry her. I just don't know if it's out of a sense of duty or because I truly care for her."

"Don't you think that's something you should figure out before you walk down the aisle?"

"If only it were that easy," he said, once again finding the rhythm of his pumping arm.

Bryan switched the weight he was using to his other hand, then took a seat on the empty bench next to Cullen's. "Look, you're not the only one who had responsibility with a capital *R* drilled into him all his life. Dad and Granddad both made sure we knew what they considered the measure of a man."

Cullen huffed out a breath. "And we saw where that got Dad, didn't we? Forced to marry when he was eighteen because he and Mom got themselves into a sticky situation."

"Isn't that the same situation you're in now?"

"Yeah," he reluctantly replied. "Which is why I'm not sure whether I'm pressing Misty to marry me because I want to be with her, or because I'm predisposed to follow in Dad's footsteps."

After lowering the heavy metal dumbbell back to its place on the weight rack, Cullen sat back, wiping sweat from his brow. "I don't want my child to grow up without a father, Bryan. I don't want to be a part-time dad, either, and I don't want Misty to be a single mother. Her life has been difficult enough without the **opportunities we've had. She works hard to support** herself and doesn't need to spend the rest of it scraping by."

"You'd never let that happen. Even if you decided not to be involved in the child's upbringing, you'd make sure they both had whatever they needed financially."

A ripple of acknowledgment skated through his belly at the truth of his brother's words. He could never stand idly by, knowing that his son or daughter was in need of something the Elliott wealth could provide.

But then, he wasn't sure he could just stand by and watch. He wanted to be there, elbow deep in dirty diapers and feeding schedules. He wanted to see his child's first smile and first steps and first time climbing on the bus to school.

"You can be a good father without marrying the child's mother, though," his brother volunteered when the silence stretched too long between them. "You can support them both, and either convince Misty to move to New York or fly out to Nevada as often as necessary to be with them and see your kid grow up."

Cullen studied his older brother from beneath lowered lashes. "What would you do if you were in my shoes?"

Bryan considered that for a second, then replaced the weight he'd been using in the only empty space left on the rack. "I guess that would depend on whether or not I was in love with the baby's mother. If not, I'd do everything I could to let my child know I loved him and was there for him. But if I was…"

He paused for emphasis and looked Cullen straight in the eye. "I'd move heaven and earth to make sure we were together."

Cullen spent the rest of the day haunted by Bryan's heartfelt statement. He had to admit, his older brother might just be wiser than he'd ever given him credit for.

The question was, was he in love with Misty or did he simply want to be a good father to their child?

When he arrived home that evening, he was no closer to finding an answer than he had been earlier, he only knew that his instincts were telling him to marry Misty, make the most of what they had together and see where the future took them. But if things didn't work out, it would be the child who suffered.

Misty greeted him at the door, looking as delectable as ever. She'd found his laundry room and mentioned that she might do a load of laundry if she started to run out of clothes. But she'd also discovered that a pair of denim shorts and one of his T-shirts made a good enough outfit to wear around the house.

He wholeheartedly agreed. Pregnancy only enhanced her already abundant curves. The jean shorts hugged her bottom and thighs, and she'd knotted the hem of his gray T-shirt to the side, offsetting the rise of her breasts and the small swell of her belly.

She looked hot…and he'd seen her both naked and in those skimpy sequined concoctions she used to wear on stage.

"How was your day?" she asked, bouncing up to take his jacket as he shrugged out of it.

"Good." He bent to place a chaste kiss on her lips. This was definitely something he could get used to—coming home at the end of a long day to her smiling face and sweet, welcoming mouth. "How about you?"

"Fine. I decided to take your advice and explore the city a little bit."

"Did you call the car service I told you about?"

"Yes." Tiny wrinkles appeared in the center of her forehead as she frowned. "I didn't want to. I thought I would call a taxi instead, but then I realized I don't have any money with me."

"The family has an account with the car service, that's why I mentioned it."

"I know, which is why I ended up going with them, after all."

His arm snaked out to catch her around the waist and draw her close.

"Then why are you still frowning?" he asked, kissing away the signs of her distress.

"Because I don't like being dependent on you for every penny I spend. I know it was your money paying for everything back in Henderson, but at least that felt different because I was teaching classes and bringing in *some* income."

"You're going to be my wife," he told her. "What's mine is yours."

If anything, that caused the lines in her brow to deepen. "I'm not going to be your wife, and I should be able to support myself and my child."

"Our child," he corrected firmly. Then his tone lightened. "Look, while you're in New York, you're my guest. I don't want you to worry about that sort of thing. If I didn't have to go into work, I'd spend every day with you, anyway. So let me leave some money for you tomorrow, along with a couple of credit cards and phone numbers, and if you need anything else, you can call me."

She gave him a look that clearly said he had missed the point.

"Humor me, would you, please?" he asked, giving her shoulders a squeeze. "We can discuss the division of assets after we're married."

Thankfully, she let the subject drop. With any other woman, he might have been suspicious, but with Misty, he knew that was just her way. If something was worth arguing about, she'd fight to the bitter end, but as far as she was concerned, some things weren't worth the effort.

"All right. Dinner's getting cold, anyway." Taking his hand, she led him through the house to the kitchen.

"You cooked?" he asked, genuinely surprised.

"Of course. Why else do you think I needed to go out today?"

When they reached the kitchen, pots were steaming on the stovetop and she released his hands to deal with them.

"Have a seat," she said, indicating the places she'd already set at the island.

He did have a dining room, which he was sure

she'd discovered during all of her alleged snooping, but the kitchen was cozier and less formal for just the two of them.

"No offense," she said, "but you were down to cocktail olives and crackers."

He winced. "Yeah, sorry. I try to keep the basics stocked, but I've been kind of distracted lately. My grandmother keeps telling me I should ask my housekeeper to shop for me, too, but I can't see the point, since I eat out more often than not or pick something up on the way home from work."

"Well, don't get too excited. This is nothing elaborate."

"It smells delicious."

He admired the smooth flow of her movements as she stirred and tasted. She strained a pan of pasta, then scooped generous portions onto two plates, covering them with red sauce. Returning to the island, she set a serving at each of their places before climbing onto her stool.

She looked so eager for his opinion of her culinary skills that he spread the linen napkin over his lap and immediately dug in. She'd added shrimp and chunks of portabello mushroom to the sauce, and flavors exploded along his taste buds.

"Mmm," he uttered in appreciation. "Very good."

She beamed at his compliment, then speared a forkful of pasta for herself. They ate in silence for several minutes before Cullen caught her eyeing **him warily.**

"What?" he asked, glancing down at his shirt front. "Did I drip?"

"No," she said on a half laugh. "I was just think-ing… If we did get married, would you expect me to be a housewife and stay-at-home mother? Cleaning the house, having dinner on the table every evening when you got home from work?"

Though the question was posed innocently enough, he sensed the seriousness behind the words. This was also the first time she'd spoken about *if* they married, rather than remaining adamant that it would never happen.

He set his fork on the side of his plate and swal-lowed, considering his answer carefully.

"I wouldn't expect anything," he told her honestly. "I would want you to do whatever made you happy. If you wanted to stay home to raise our children, that would be fine with me. And if you enjoyed cleaning or cooking, that would be fine, too. But I have a housekeeper, and we could also hire a cook, if you wanted, so it wouldn't have to be an issue."

"What if I wanted to work outside of the house?"

"I'd be okay with that, too. Misty," he said, stretching his arm across the corner of the island to squeeze her hand, "whatever you want to do with your life, I'll be agreeable. Within reason, of course," he added, flashing her a grin. "I don't know how thrilled I'd be with the idea of you jumping out of air-planes or running into burning buildings. But if you wanted a position at EPH, I'd do whatever I could to get you a job there. If you wanted to teach dance at Juilliard, I'd support you on that, too."

"Juilliard," she scoffed, rolling her eyes. "Right. Like they would want a former Las Vegas showgirl on their faculty."

"You're a great dancer, Misty. You worked as a showgirl, but we both know you're talented at other forms of dance, too. You could wipe the floor with those Juilliard stiffs, if you wanted to."

When she beamed at him, it made all the moments of doubt and disappointment at her rejections fade away. He understood now—at least in part—why she continued to turn him down.

She felt out of her element. The thought of marrying him scared her because she considered herself not good enough for an Elliott, far from socialite material.

He hated that she thought so little of herself. If she only knew how much the Elliott family needed her—how much *he* needed her—to add a spark to their lives and loosen up some of the rigidity Patrick Elliott had drilled into all of them from infancy.

His mind flashed back to his brother's remarks that afternoon at the EPH gym. Bryan was right. He needed to decide if his proposals to Misty were based on emotion or an ingrained sense of responsibility.

He was beginning to believe it was the former. *Love* might be too strong a word. After all, he'd never been in love and wasn't quite sure how a sensation like that would feel. But he cared for her deeply. So much so that he wanted to marry her, raise their child together, spend the rest of his life with her.

He *wanted* those things, he realized. He wasn't selflessly offering to take them upon his shoulders because it was the decent and respectable thing to do.

They finished the rest of their meals in a comfortable silence, but when Misty rose to carry the dishes to the dishwasher, Cullen wiped his mouth with his napkin, knowing he needed to ask one more time.

"Hey, Misty?"

She acknowledged him without turning around, her light brown hair with those streaks of blond falling over her shoulder and back as she bent to fill the bottom rack.

His throat closed for a minute, the words sticking as his chest tightened and a wave of unexpected emotion washed over him. He'd asked her to marry him a dozen times before, but for some reason, he suspected this time was different. This time, her refusal just might crush him.

He swallowed hard, his fingers turning white as they clutched the edge of the island. "Will you marry me?"

She stopped what she was doing and turned to meet his gaze. Sadness and regret flashed through her eyes for a split second, and he knew what was coming.

"I'm sorry, Cullen, the answer is still no."

Ten

Two days later, Misty was wandering around Cullen's town house, trying to find something interesting to occupy her time. She'd already straightened the kitchen and bedroom, flipped through channels on the television in the living room and read the first few chapters of a popular fiction paperback she'd found in the den.

It wasn't even noon and she was bored already. Cullen had assured her she wouldn't be expected to be a housewife or stay-at-home mom. She could go out if she wanted, find a job or other activity to keep occupied.

If she married him. Which she wouldn't. Couldn't, no matter how much her heart might protest the decision of her better judgment.

She would still see him. He would come to Nevada to visit his child, and she was sure he'd ask her to fly east with the baby a few times a year. They could spend time together then.

Things might not be the same between them—their sexual relationship would likely transform itself into something more platonic—but at least he would still be in her life. She wouldn't lose him completely just because she refused to love, honor and cherish him.

She didn't need vows for that. She already felt all of those things and more for him. But she wouldn't intrude upon his life, forcing him to make room for her and a child when she was sure that had been as far from his plans as flying to the moon.

It hadn't exactly been in her plans, either, but she could incorporate the role of single mother into her everyday life much more easily than he could incorporate a pregnant ex-showgirl into his.

With a sigh, she plopped down on the sofa in front of the TV, contemplating another run through the channels to see if anything interesting had come on in the past ten minutes. She could go out—it was a balmy May afternoon—but had already done about as much exploring as she cared to do on her own. Or maybe…maybe she should think about going back to Las Vegas.

Back to her dance studio and normal routine. She might not be able to teach classes quite the way she had in the past, but there were adjustments that could be made to allow her studio to remain open. A couple of the students had been taking classes from her long enough to pick up the slack and demonstrate moves she was no longer capable of.

And there was no sense dragging out the inevitable. She would have to return home eventually. Maybe sooner would be better than later, especially considering the tension that had developed between Cullen and her ever since that night in the kitchen when he'd asked her one more time to marry him.

One last time, it seemed, since he hadn't broached the subject again.

Where he used to propose several times a day, it had now been several days since the topic of marriage had even been discussed. They still made love, still slept in each other's arms and he still called from work to check on her. But what he didn't do was ask her to marry him morning, noon and night.

She missed it, she thought with a pang low in her belly. As many times as she'd turned him down, it was horrible of her to be sorry he'd stopped, but she was. She missed the tiny thrill of anticipation that used to sing through her veins every time the phone rang or he walked through the door.

She'd said no because it was the right thing to do, but it had been flattering to hear him pose the question over and over, as though he really meant it.

When the doorbell chimed, her heart lurched and she jumped to her feet, thinking it might be Cullen. A second later, her senses returned and she realized he would simply use his key, not ring the bell.

Still, a visitor would be a nice distraction. She almost didn't care if it was a door-to-door salesperson wanting to demonstrate the amazing power of a new vacuum cleaner, or a neighbor looking for her toy poodle.

What she didn't expect to find when she pulled open the door was Cullen's cousin Bridget. Misty hadn't seen the woman since their amusing and slightly embarrassing encounter in his office a couple of weeks ago, but that didn't keep her from stepping into the foyer and greeting Misty with a wide, bright smile.

"Hi, there," Bridget said enthusiastically, tossing her lime green handbag over one shoulder. "I hope I'm not intruding."

Misty shook her head. She hadn't even gotten the chance to say hello, but was beginning to realize this was probably typical of encounters with Bridget. The young woman was energetic almost to a fault, and brought a smile to Misty's lips without even trying.

She was wearing an orange sleeveless top with a small tie holding together the two sides of the deep V-neck. Her skirt had an angled hem and a swirl design that incorporated the same colors of her blouse, purse and brown shoes. Her dark blond shoulder-length hair was pulled back on either side with rhinestone clips that sparkled in the sunlight shining through the front windows.

"I'm so glad." A determined light played across her blue eyes. "Now tell me you don't have plans for the day."

Misty shook her head again. "No. Why?"

Bridget released what must have been a pent-up breath. "Great, because I came to take you to lunch."

"Excuse me?" Misty blinked, feeling somewhat disconcerted.

"Lunch. You know, the meal between breakfast and dinner. The activity in which women get together for a little gossip and girl talk."

She flashed a grin and moved forward to squeeze Misty's arm. "Come on. I know Cullen is at work and you must be going stir-crazy cooped up here by yourself. We'll go out, grab a bite and I'll fill you in on all the best need-to-know about the Elliott clan. You can ask me how to get on Granddad's good side—if he even *has* a good side—" she added with a roll of her eyes, "and what Cullen was like as a kid."

That last was icing on the cake. Misty had been almost desperate to find something to do, and since she liked Bridget immensely, going out to lunch with her sounded like fun. But now that she'd mentioned it, Misty did want to know more about Cullen's childhood and the man who would be her child's great-grandfather.

"Let me just grab my purse," she said, turning to head upstairs. "I should probably phone Cullen, too, to let him know I won't be home for a while."

"He already knows," Bridget called after her.

Misty paused halfway up the steps.

"I told him what I was up to before I left EPH. He said we should enjoy ourselves and bring him some leftovers." Bridget crossed her arms over her chest. "As if. Let him find his own food. If we talk as long as I think we will, we may still be out at dinnertime."

Misty chuckled before running the rest of the way to the bedroom to retrieve her small clutch purse. When they stepped outside, she noticed Bridget had a Town Car from the same service Cullen had recommended waiting at the curb.

"I'm not allowed to let you overdo it," Bridget said as they slipped into the air conditioned backseat.

"I feel fine," Misty felt the need to put in.

"I'm sure you do, but Cullen told us about your hospital stay—scared ten years off of him, I'd venture to say—and he just doesn't want you getting sick or risking the baby. You're lucky he doesn't have you on bed rest, whether the doctor suggested it or not," she said with a wink. "The Elliotts are like that—stubborn, determined know-it-alls."

"You included?" Misty asked with a small smile.

"Of course." Bridget didn't seem the least offended or put off by the description. "As much as I hate it sometimes—especially Granddad—I'm lucky I was born into this family. Anyone else's and they'd have probably tied me up in a burlap sack and tossed me into the East River years ago. As it is, they consider me hell on wheels. Most of the time, I think they all stand back and hope that if I do anything really stupid, I won't take them down with me."

"It must be nice to belong to such a large, close-knit family."

"It is," Bridget replied without hesitation. "It can be a pain in the butt, too, but any time I'm in trouble or need something, I know I can turn to them."

A beat passed before Bridget said, "You can, too, you know. Once you and Cullen get married, you'll be as much an Elliott as the rest of us and can come to me or the others whenever you need anything."

Misty started to protest that she and Cullen weren't going to marry, then thought better of it. He had probably already told his family they were, and no amount of argument from her would convince them differently.

Besides, she really didn't want to bring Cullen's cousin into the debate. It would become clear enough to everyone that a wedding wasn't going to take place when no plans were made and she flew back to Las Vegas.

She also took exception to the idea that she would fold naturally into their family and automatically become *one of them* just because she married Cullen. Bridget herself had said that their grandfather, Patrick Elliott, had been overheard claiming, *no grandson of mine is going to marry a stripper!*

She wasn't a stripper and never had been, but doubted the eldest Elliott would appreciate the distinction.

A lot of people felt the same way, so she could hardly blame him for the misconception. It bothered her more that he had apparently made up his mind about her and her relationship with Cullen before even meeting her. But then, she couldn't blame him for that, either. In his shoes, she probably would have had a similar reaction.

From the outside, she was sure she looked like a gold digger, out for the Elliott money. An ex-showgirl, searching for a way out of Las Vegas and into one of the wealthiest and most successful families in the northeast.

First, they would say, she lured Cullen in with hot sex and a convenient affair. Then she managed to get herself pregnant and trap him into a loveless marriage.

If only people—Cullen's family included—knew the truth. How much she really did care for him, and that this pregnancy had been as much of a shock to her as it had to anyone else.

Her hand moved to cover the slight bulge in her lap as the Town Car moved through the stop-and-go Manhattan traffic.

That was another reason she couldn't marry Cullen—because no matter what they did or said, no one would ever believe she hadn't gotten pregnant on purpose to tie him to her and gain ready access to his money.

She might be a kept woman, but she wasn't a gold digger and didn't think she could live with the knowledge that everyone in the world thought she was.

Hours later, Misty and Bridget sat at a white latticework table on the patio of a local delicatessen. A slight breeze ruffled the umbrella over their heads as they made slow work of their sandwiches and fruit salad.

They probably would have been at the restaurant much earlier, except that Bridget had insisted they stop along the way. After hearing about what Misty had done so far on her first visit to New York, she had declared Misty's outings boring and pedestrian and decided to give her a taste of what the Elliott women considered a fun day of shopping.

She had taken Misty to several jewelry stores and boutiques, encouraging her to buy something at each. She kept telling her *he wouldn't mind,* and a part of Misty knew it was true. But she felt extremely uncomfortable at the notion of making or asking Cullen to pay for anything more than necessities for her.

Providing for their child was one thing, but she refused to accept baubles and superfluous gifts that would make her feel like more than just a mistress. They would make her feel like a whore. No better than the type of woman everyone already assumed her to be.

She didn't say as much to Bridget, even though she suspected the woman would have understood if she'd explained. Instead, Bridget had shrugged one slim shoulder each time Misty declined to make a purchase and went ahead to buy a hat and pair of calf-high boots for herself.

On and off while they strolled through the shops and rode through town in the luxury sedan, Bridget filled her in on all kinds of family gossip and the goings-on at EPH.

Some of it made her laugh, such as the story Bridget told of one of *The Buzz* employees attending a meeting with the word *Urgent* stamped across the back of his rumpled shirt, giving everyone a pretty clear idea of what he'd been up to in the copy room with one of the magazine's young receptionists.

Other parts made her wonder, like the apparent competition Patrick Elliott had set up between his children by issuing the challenge that whichever one of them made the biggest success of his or her magazine by the end of the year would be given the position of CEO of EPH when Patrick retired.

Misty couldn't imagine pitting siblings against one another in any manner, let alone over something as inconsequential as a family business. She realized how large an empire EPH was, but it was still just a company, just a job, not nearly as important as family and children, love and respect.

Hearing such a thing about the man who would be her own child's great-grandfather made her feel slightly ill. She wasn't particularly looking forward to meeting Patrick, but she swore that no matter what, she would protect their child from him and his gruff demeanor, his disdain—or outright hatred, as the case may be—and his manipulative personality.

"He's a controlling old bastard, is what he is," Bridget told her, munching on her sandwich as she continued on the topic of her grandfather. "His interference in my life and the rest of the family's lives drives me insane. Somebody needs to either shake some sense into him or tell him to leave us the hell alone."

Misty sipped at the glass of cranberry juice she'd ordered with her meal, nodding in agreement. She certainly didn't have anything to offer other than her own personal concerns about how Patrick would affect her and her baby's life, and Bridget seemed content to have a captive audience while she talked.

"He made Uncle Daniel marry Aunt Amanda when she got pregnant right out of high school. And I guess we should all be grateful or we wouldn't have Cullen to love." She shot Misty a knowing, lopsided grin. "But they still should have been allowed to make up their own minds about how to handle the situation. They might have ended up together anyway, and then wouldn't have gotten divorced. Even if they wouldn't have, I'd bet you anything Daniel still would have been a great father and done right by both Amanda and Bryan."

She washed down the sandwich with a gulp of soda. "And forcing Finola to give up her baby when she got pregnant at fifteen was just *wrong*. I mean, I don't think poor Aunt Finny has ever gotten over it. She's let her job as editor in chief of *Charisma* completely take over her life. She won't even date."

Leaning back in her chair, Bridget added, "I don't want the magazine to take over my whole life, that's for sure."

A second later, she leaned forward again and whispered conspiratorially, "If I tell you something, will you promise not to breathe a word of it to anyone? Not even Cullen?"

Misty sat in stunned silence for a moment. She felt both honored that Cullen's cousin wanted to confide in her and unworthy at the same time. But she nodded, anyway, stretching over her plate to hear what Bridget had to say, because she was loathe to put an end to the camaraderie she'd found with this young woman.

"Cross your heart?" Bridget demanded.

"Cross my heart…" she promised, forming the invisible symbol on the front of her shirt.

"I love running the photo department at *Charisma,* don't get me wrong. And I've never told this to anyone before, but… I've been working on a tell-all book about the Elliott family. Granddad would *die* if he knew. As it is, he'll probably kill me when he finds out. But it has to be done. Somebody has to let the world know what kind of man Patrick Elliott really is and what he's done to get where he is."

Almost before Misty had a chance to digest all that, Bridget's expression went from harshly determined to soft and unsure.

She huffed out a breath and shoved a wedge of cantaloupe in her mouth. "Do you think I'm crazy? Do you think I'm risking not only my grandfather's wrath, but my entire family's rejection?"

"I don't know," Misty answered honestly. She didn't know any of them, save Cullen, well enough to predict how they would react to Bridget's clandestine actions or to a tome that would reveal to the world the inner workings and private scandals of the Elliott family dynasty.

"I think…" She took a deep breath and then dove in with her honest opinion. "I think you need to do what feels right to you. It sounds like you're very passionate about this project, and I can only think that's a good thing. You shouldn't spend your life working at a job you don't love or doing something that makes you feel unfulfilled."

She took another sip of juice before bravely forging on. "Just because you write this book doesn't mean you have to seek publication for it. You could do it for your own satisfaction and no one else would ever need to know."

At that, Bridget's face fell. It was obvious her aspirations for this tell-all were much larger than simply a secret hobby.

"But if you do publish it… I'm not an Elliott, so maybe I shouldn't even be saying this, but maybe airing out some of the family linens is exactly what your grandfather needs to realize he's been too controlling of his children and grandchildren."

"Really?" Bridget reached across the glass-topped table and squeezed Misty's hand. "Oh, Misty, thank you. That makes me feel so much better. At least you understand. Someone has to be brave enough to tell the truth about the Elliott family—not just the truth as Patrick Elliott has concocted it."

The rest of their lunch passed without any more

heavy disclosures, but Misty still felt herself withdrawing emotionally. She liked Bridget very much, but knew that forging too much of a friendship with her would be unfair when she probably wouldn't be in town much longer and might never return to New York after that.

When they pulled up in front of Cullen's town house, Bridget immediately leaned across the seat to embrace Misty before she could step out of the car. Misty hugged her back, her eyes stinging with tears as she realized she'd finally met someone with whom she could truly become friends.

And that she might never see the young woman again.

Eleven

"How was your lunch with Bridget?"

Misty was sitting at the kitchen island, staring at, but not really solving, the crossword puzzle from yesterday's paper.

She raised her head at Cullen's question, realizing she hadn't heard him come in. Hadn't heard the front door open…his footsteps across the hardwood floor…his keys hitting the hall credenza. He'd shrugged out of his suit jacket and set down his briefcase, but she hadn't heard or witnessed those actions, either.

And it was no great mystery why. Spending the afternoon with Bridget had filled her mind with a million different thoughts, all of them centering on

Cullen and whether or not she should risk staying with him in New York any longer.

Scratching her head in a distracted gesture, she pasted a smile on her face that she didn't quite feel and twisted around on her stool.

"Good. I like your cousin," she answered. "How about you? How was your day?"

"Good."

He continued forward until he stood directly in front of her, hedging her in, his breath dancing over her cheeks, her lashes, her lips. Lifting his hands, he set his palms against the edge of the island on either side of her and leaned in.

"I missed you, though. I was thinking," he murmured, his mouth grazing her temple, them moving down along the line of her jaw, "maybe tomorrow you could come into work with me. That way, whenever I start daydreaming about you, you'll be right there instead of so far away."

The corners of her lips turned up in amusement at his exaggeration of the distance between his office and his house.

"Wouldn't that be distracting for you?" she asked, driving her fingers through his hair and letting her head fall back as he kissed a molten path down the column of her neck.

"Not half as distracting as it's been wanting you and not having you in easy reach."

Her heart gave a little flip at his words, and her toes curled inside her shoes.

She wanted to ask if he'd found her equally distracting for the past four years, while they'd been carrying on their affair, living at opposite ends of the country. But she was too afraid of what his response might be. Too afraid he hadn't thought of her much at all, while she'd thought of him each and every day.

His nose nuzzled the scoop neck of her shirt just above her breasts, his tongue darting out to wet her rapidly heating skin. Her eyes slid closed and a low purr sounded at the back of her throat.

"Let's go upstairs," Cullen growled.

"Aren't you hungry? Don't you want dinner first?"

He straightened and her eyes popped open. Before she could guess his intent, he scooped her up in his arms and turned for the foyer.

"The only thing I'm hungry for right now is you. Food can wait."

He took the stairs quickly but carefully, moving toward the bedroom like a man on a mission. When he reached the foot of the bed, he laid her gently atop the mattress and followed her down.

The look in his eyes was intense, possessive... adoring, and it caused her stomach to clench with regret. She would miss him so much when she left.

And she would leave. She had to. But it would be one of the hardest things she'd ever had to do. Because she loved him.

Deep down in her soul, she knew she always had. All the denials and claims that she was in the affair because he was a good man and treated her better than any of the guys from her past were just so much smoke.

She loved him in a way she hadn't known possible, and for the first time thanked God she was carrying his child. It might be selfish of her to think it, but at least by having his baby, she would always have a piece of him, always have a connection to him that no one and nothing could break.

If she could, she would marry him, spend the rest of her life with him. But that would require her to have been working as something other than a showgirl when they met, and for their relationship to have begun as something other than an illicit, red-hot affair.

His being an Elliott didn't help, either. Maybe if he weren't, then some of the hurdles between them wouldn't have looked quite so insurmountable.

Moisture prickled behind her eyes and she bit the inside of her lip, blinking rapidly to keep her emotions in check. If Cullen noticed she was close to tears, he would want to know what was wrong, and wouldn't let up until she told him.

But how could she tell him that she was leaving him because she loved him? Tell him and make him understand that it was for the best—for everyone.

She knew Cullen would try to talk her out of it. When that didn't work, he would try to argue her into changing her mind. And if she was still determined to go, he would likely tie her to the bed until she came to her senses.

A smile tugged at the corners of her mouth. His

stubborn streak and single-mindedness were two of the things she loved most about him. They made her feel cared for and protected.

But this time, she couldn't let his Elliott arrogance stop her from doing what she knew was right.

Brushing his thumbs over the twin arches of her brows, he stared down at her, his body pressed along hers from shoulder to ankle.

"You look so serious," he said softly. "What are you thinking?"

The words *I love you* were on the tip of her tongue, but she couldn't let them escape.

For one thing, love hadn't been part of the agreement when they'd first started sleeping together; it wouldn't be fair for her to bring such a sentiment into the deal now.

For another, she couldn't bear to tell Cullen she loved him and not hear the words in return. Or worse, to see his face turn stony and tense as he tried to figure out a way to extricate himself from a mistress who had suddenly become too clingy and emotionally involved.

Pregnancy or no pregnancy, shared child or no shared child, she had to remember that they were still only a mister and mistress.

She shook her head, raising her arms to run her fingers through his silky hair.

"Nothing important," she answered in response to his question, pushing all other thoughts and feelings to the back of her mind. "I was just thinking about how nice it is to be someone's substitution for food and drink."

"Not someone's," he growled. "Mine."

His teeth closed on the muscle in her throat, over the jugular vein, in predatory possessiveness. Her pulse sped up, pumping blood even harder past the area where his hot, wet tongue now swirled against her skin. She writhed beneath him, wanting closer, wanting more.

He released her throat and moved to her mouth, kissing her with a heat and passion that sucked the air from her lungs and left her breathless.

While his tongue parried with her own, his hands caressed her arms, her waist, her breasts.

Little by little she felt her clothes loosen and begin to fall away. Rolling and shifting, she let him strip the black slacks and hot pink top from her body, leaving her in only panties and bra.

Returning the favor, she slipped the end of his tie through its knot and pulled the entire length away from his collar. Next, she slowly ran her fingers down the front of his shirt, releasing each of the small buttons until the material gaped open, leaving his broad, smooth chest bare to her touch.

He inhaled sharply, his abdomen going rigid as her nails trailed along his sides and into the waistband of his dress pants. She flipped the catch open with her thumb and forefinger, easing the zipper down as she continued to drink from his lips, nipping, licking, sucking.

When she delved into his briefs to gently cup his straining erection, Cullen pulled away and jumped to his feet to shed his shoes and trousers so quickly, she chuckled. He came back to her blessedly naked and wasted no time freeing her from the constriction of her matching bra and panties.

Their mouths met. Breaths mingled and limbs tangled as they twisted and rolled around on top of the bedclothes. He kissed the side of her neck, drew the lobe of her ear into his mouth, then his lips moved lower, across her chest, until they reached the peak of one breast.

He circled the budded nipple before pulling it into his mouth, at the same time using the pad of his thumb to tease and torment the tip of her other breast.

She arched her back, pressing into the sensations he stirred to life, straining for relief as the pressure built and pulsed through her, gathering force at her very core.

Misty pulled her legs up, wrapping them around his waist, and he slid into her easily in one fluid stroke. Her muscles clutched at him automatically, making her gasp as pleasure washed over her like an ocean wave.

Her fingers played along his back, his shoulders, the planes of his chest. His jaw tightened, the cords of his neck standing out in stark relief as his hips flexed, pounding into her again and again.

The world ceased to exist, narrowing to a pinpoint of space and time where only the two of them existed, in this room, at this moment. All other thoughts and concerns disappeared. The air filled with the sounds of heavy breathing and moans of intense pleasure.

Cullen's hands stroked down her sides, one coming to flex and rest on her hip while the other delved into the folds of her slick, swollen sex. His thumb sought and found the bud of her desire, and pressed, shooting lightning bolts of pure ecstasy through every pore and cell of her body.

Her back arched, her heels dug in, and her nails curled into his shoulders as she came with a long keening cry. Leaning in even closer, Cullen continued to thrust, continued to rub and tease her so that the spasms rocking her body went on and on. And then he stiffened, pouring into her with a heartfelt groan.

When her heart had stopped pounding in her chest like a marching band on parade, Misty opened her eyes to find Cullen staring down at her with those stark blue eyes. He held himself above her, away from the mound of her belly, his arms straining with the effort.

And then he grinned, leaning forward to press a firm, satisfied kiss to her mouth before rolling to his side. "I don't know about you, but I'll take that kind of meal over boring old meatloaf any day."

Even as her eyes drifted closed, her lips curved in agreement. "Mmm."

Pulling the sheets and comforter loose from beneath them, he covered them both to their chests and snuggled up to her.

They were on their sides, with him pressed behind her, spoon fashion. His arm was curled around her waist, his lips brushing her neck and shoulder.

Dragging in a deep breath, she tried not to let it stutter back out as she exhaled. She didn't want him to know she was crying. If he realized, he would want to know why and would pressure her with questions she didn't have answers to.

His fingers played absently along the taut, bare flesh of her protruding stomach, which only made her heart lurch and her throat clog with emotion.

He was such a good man, and there was nothing she wanted more than to lie here with him every night for the rest of their lives. To know that she belonged to him…with him…that a future together shone brightly before them.

But she didn't, and she knew what she had to do. No matter how much it might hurt.

Twelve

When Cullen arrived home from work the next day, he found himself whistling as he took the front steps two at a time.

That's what a good woman could do for you, he decided. Make you feel like skipping even after a long, hard day. Make you eager to get home and do more than pop a single serving frozen meal into the microwave or crash in front of the TV for a few hours before crawling upstairs to bed.

It bothered him that she wouldn't marry him, there was no doubting that. In fact, if he were honest, he'd have to admit it was more along the lines of crushed.

He'd never asked anyone to marry him before. Never cared enough about any woman to ask.

But he cared about Misty. And he cared about their unborn child.

He wanted her to be his wife, dammit. But he'd asked…at least a hundred times. And she'd turned him down…at least a hundred times.

He didn't know what more he could do to convince her, short of tossing her over his shoulder and carrying her off somewhere to perform Chinese water torture until she gave in.

Which left him with only one final option: take what he could get. She wouldn't agree to marry him, but she seemed happy enough to live with him here in New York.

So that was what they'd do. It might not be ideal, and his family might not offer their one hundred percent approval, but it could work.

They could live together and raise the baby together. Just one big, happy family, even without the sanctity of marriage.

His gut clenched at the idea; his fingers tightened on the front door handle.

He'd always been the playboy of the family, with pretty women hanging on his arm and his every word. His bed had only been empty when he wanted it to be.

So why did it suddenly feel imperative that he tie the knot, not just shack up with Misty?

Because they were having a child together?

Because she was the one woman for whom he was willing to give up all other women?

He honestly didn't know. He'd asked himself the

same questions numerous times but still didn't have the answers.

But vows or no vows, they could still make it work. They *would* make it work. He would see to it.

Pushing the door open, he stepped inside the town house, cocked his head and listened for signs of Misty. He often found her in the kitchen, throwing together something for dinner. Or in the sitting room, reading a book.

He set down his briefcase and shrugged out of his suit jacket, then made his way down the hall. He didn't smell anything coming from the kitchen, but that didn't mean she wasn't in there.

When he reached the back of the house, however, the room was empty. No pots or pans heating on the stove, no place settings laid out on the kitchen island.

He checked the living room next, and then the den. His brows knit as the first niggling sense of concern started to tickle at the base of his spine.

It probably shouldn't worry him that Misty wasn't downstairs when he arrived, but it did. Only because she always had been before. And because she was pregnant and had had complications before.

These days, he seemed to carry a pocket of constant fear and concern with him everywhere he went. Concern for Misty's health and safety. Fear that something could happen to send her to the hospital again and that she might lose the baby.

He tamped down those worries on a daily basis, not wanting her to know that impending fatherhood had turned him into a writhing mass of raw nerve endings and quivering gelatinous goo.

She was fine, he told himself, but hurried up the stairs to the second floor, just in case.

"Misty?" He called her name, expecting an immediate response. Instead, his query was met with silence.

Perhaps she was in the shower. Or taking a nap. He understood that pregnant women got tired easily and needed extra rest.

When he got to the bedroom, he found the door ajar and quickly stretched out an arm to push it open the rest of the way.

Instead of finding Misty in bed, he saw her standing beside the king-size mattress, folding clothes and packing them neatly inside her open suitcase.

Cullen stood in the doorway, frozen in place by the sight before him. The blood in his veins turned thick and sluggish. His brain strained to function, but failed.

"Hey," he forced past his tongue, which felt twice as large as normal inside his mouth.

Her movements halted and she slowly turned her head, meeting his gaze. The sadness in her eyes slammed into his solar plexus like a fist. But what drove the air from his lungs and made the room spin around him was the determination written plainly on her face.

"What are you doing?" he asked, afraid he already knew the answer.

She turned back to her task, finished folding a pair of black slacks and tucked them into the luggage. "I'm packing."

"I can see that. Where are we going?" he asked, striving for levity, praying his suspicions weren't valid.

"*We're* not going anywhere," she said. "*I'm* going home."

Oh, God. "This is your home."

"No, Cullen," she said softly. "This is *your* home. My home is in Nevada."

That was enough to get his blood pumping again, followed by a quick surge of panicked annoyance. He strode across the room, reaching her in three long strides, and grabbed her arm before she could pick up the next item of clothing.

"Your home is with me," he told her firmly. "Where we live is irrelevant."

"Cullen…"

She pulled her arm away, and he let her go. Her lashes fanned across her cheeks as her gaze floated to the floor, then back up again.

"I'm sorry, but this isn't going to work. I appreciate everything you've done and everything you've tried to do these past weeks."

Her fingers rubbed absently along the edge of the suitcase while she struggled to keep her eyes locked with his.

"And you know I won't try to keep you from the baby—that isn't even an issue. But I can't stay here any longer, pretending to be something I'm not…pretending *we're* something we're not."

"No one asked you to be anything but who you are."

She shook her head, sending her brown and blond

hair swinging around her shoulders. "You want me to be your wife, when I am definitely not Elliott material. Your grandfather wants me to be a social-ite instead of a dancer, when I'm well past the age of being molded into someone I'm not."

A fine sheen of perspiration broke out along his skin, slid down his back and turned his palms damp with apprehension. He could feel her slipping away from him, and was damned if he knew how to stop it.

"To hell with what Granddad wants," he growled brutally. "To hell with what I want, for that matter. What do *you* want?"

Her breasts rose as she drew a deep breath, then gave a heartfelt sigh. "I want to go back to the way things were. I'm not sorry about the baby," she said, laying a protective hand on her belly, "but you have to admit it's complicated our lives. I won't complicate your life any longer, though. That's why I'm leaving."

Complicate his life? Didn't she know she made his life *better?* That she was like a rainbow after a summer storm…a roaring fire on a cold winter day…his soft place to fall when everything else around him was a whirlwind of stress and confusion?

She'd been the one constant in his life, from almost the moment they had met. Always welcom-ing him with open arms, ready and willing to listen and accept him as he was.

How could she not know that?

How could she not know he loved her?

The truth slammed into him, stealing his breath and nearly sending him staggering backward.

He loved her. It was so simple. So obvious, he couldn't believe he hadn't realized it sooner.

He didn't just find her attractive, wasn't only interested in her body. And he didn't want to be with her simply because she was pregnant with his child.

He wanted that child, but he wanted her, too. Wanted her as his wife, his lover, his partner from now until the day they died.

It was no wonder he hadn't been able to give her up over the years. Regardless of the other women who'd passed through his life or the number of times he'd told himself he should break things off with Misty, he never could, and now he knew why.

He had been in love with her all along. Deep down, in a place even he hadn't known existed.

"Misty."

His voice broke on her name, but he wasn't embarrassed. He was shocked, amazed...ecstatic. He wanted to grab her up and squeeze her tight, swing her around and shout at the top of his lungs about his newfound revelation.

"Why now?" he asked instead. "I thought you were happy here, that *we* were happy here, and you were enjoying getting to know my family. What happened to change your mind?"

Her gaze skittered away from his own and she turned back to her packing. This time he let her go, more eager to hear her answer than hold her undivided attention.

"Nothing happened," she said. "I just realized that I've been here longer than I planned and need to get back to the studio and my classes."

He didn't believe her, but wasn't going to press the point. It didn't really matter, anyway.

"What if I told you I love you?" he blurted out almost desperately.

Her movements halted, a pair of panties hung limply from her fingers. As though in slow motion, her body twisted around until she was facing him once again. Her eyes were wide, the muscles in her throat convulsing as she swallowed hard.

"What did you say?"

He stepped forward. His face split, he was sure, with a goofy grin. His hands closed on her upper arms, his thumbs stroked her in a reassuring caress.

"I love you, Misty. I think I always have." He lifted a hand to stroke her cheek and comb his fingers through her hair. "You were never just a mistress to me. From the moment I met you, I knew you were more than that. I may not have been willing to admit it at the time…"

He gave a harsh laugh. "Hell, I may not have been willing to admit it now, except that I'm scared to death about losing you."

His fingers flexed on her bare skin. "I don't want you to go," he told her simply. "But if you feel you have to…if Nevada is where you really want to be, then I'll go with you."

"Cullen—"

"I'll leave EPH if I have to. Or find a way to work for the family long-distance. I don't care, as long as we're together."

She shook her head, blinking rapidly as her gorgeous green eyes glittered with unshed tears.

"I can't, Cullen," she said, her voice clouded with emotion. Twin drops of moisture formed on her lashes before spilling over to streak down her cheeks. "I love you, too, but I don't want to be the reason you eventually come to hate me."

His heart kicked into a gallop. He was so delighted by her admission of being in love with him, too, that at first he didn't catch the rest of her pronouncement.

When he did, his smile slipped and he started to get that sick, slick feeling in his gut again.

"What are you talking about?" he asked, thoroughly perplexed. He couldn't imagine anything she might do or say to ever cause him to hate her.

"I'm not the right woman for you. You need a wife you can be proud of, one your family will approve of. Not a mistress you felt obligated to marry just because she got pregnant."

She sniffed, valiantly wiping the tears from her face only to have more fall in their place. "I know you feel responsible for me and the baby, and that you want to do the right thing by us because it's what your father and grandfather have raised you to do. But I won't be another duty you feel compelled to fulfill, and neither will this child."

Cullen could only stare at her, stunned by her words. He did think of her and the baby as his responsibility, but because he *loved* them, not because he felt trapped or obligated. Where would she have gotten the idea that—?

His crossed brows began to lift, the corners of his mouth moving from their downward tilt into a lopsided grin.

"Bridget," he breathed, not sure whether he should be furious or amused.

Shaking his head, he said, "Bridget filled your head with stories about how my father and then my brother and I were raised, didn't she? Told you all about Granddad and how overbearing he can be, always drilling into us that an Elliott takes responsibility for his actions. Am I right?"

She started to nod, but he didn't need even that much confirmation.

"I love my cousin, but the next time I see her, I swear I'm going to wring her neck," he muttered.

"Listen to me, Misty."

He ran his hands up her arms, over her shoulders, until they came to rest on the slope of her long, slim neck. His fingers dug gently into the base of her skull, his thumbs framing her jawline.

"I love you. I love our baby. You are not an obligation to me, a duty. You are a gift. A blessing I didn't even know I needed until you came into my life. And I'll thank God every day for the rest of my life that you did. I never want to spend another moment apart from you."

Closing his eyes, he lowered his head until their foreheads touched, then he opened his eyes again and stared directly into those deep emerald pools he hoped he would be lucky enough to gaze into for the rest of his life.

"Marry me, Misty. We'll live anywhere you want, do anything you want. Just marry me. *Please.*"

Misty inhaled a deep, ragged breath, her heart beating so hard behind her rib cage, she knew he must be able to feel it against his own chest. Tears continued to roll down her cheeks, but they'd transformed into tears of happiness rather than tears of sadness and regret.

There wasn't a doubt in her mind that Cullen meant what he said. He *didn't* think of her as a responsibility to be handled with a stiff upper lip.

And most importantly, he *loved* her. As much as she loved him.

Clearing her throat, she opened her mouth, hoping her voice would work—now, when she needed it more than ever.

"I remember the first night I met you, when you came backstage after the show," she said softly, touching his handsome, familiar face, so dear to her, with the tips of her fingers. "I knew from that very moment that my life would never be the same."

Pressing her mouth to his, she let her eyes slide closed for a brief moment before opening them and whispering against his lips, "Yes. I'll marry you."

He pulled back, only slightly, and she watched the

smile form on his face, growing wider until pleasure filled his gaze from the inside out.

"Finally," he breathed, then wrapped his arms around her and hugged her tight.

"You've made me a very happy man," he said just above her ear. "I promise you won't be sorry."

She laid her cheek on his shoulder, her nails curling into the material of his tailored brown suit jacket. "You're sure it doesn't bother you I'm five years older than you are, or that everyone will know you married an ex-showgirl?"

"Are you kidding me?" he returned.

He shot her a wide, wicked grin and added a wink that made her toes curl inside her pretty pastel slides.

"Older women make better lovers. That's what the song says, right? I happen to know whoever wrote it is one hundred percent on the money. And as for you being a former showgirl…if anyone gets on my case, I'll simply explain that you can cross your ankles behind her head. They'll not only understand, they'll beg me to introduce them to some of your dancer friends."

They both knew the situation was more serious than that, but she buried her face in his chest and laughed, anyway. His sense of humor was another one of the traits she loved best about him, so as long as he could hold on to it through thick and thin, she really believed they would be all right.

"And your grandfather…?" she ventured.

"Granddad will learn to accept you. And if he doesn't, then he'll learn to keep his mouth shut or he won't be allowed to see his first great-grandchild."

"Oh, no, Cullen—"

He covered her mouth with two fingers. "Don't worry," he said. "We'll work it out. Whatever it is, we'll work through it *together*. Together, okay?"

"Together," she whispered, and they sealed the deal with a kiss.

Thirteen

Two weeks later

Cullen stood outside the Tides, the Elliott family's palatial estate in the Hamptons, tugging at the bow tie of his black tuxedo. The darn thing was all but cutting off his circulation.

And his brother was late, dammit.

Everyone else was inside, flowers were arranged, his family and the minister were present, guests were seated. Only Bryan—his best man—had yet to show up.

Even to the casual observer, Cullen would probably look nervous. And considering that it was his wedding day, he figured he had every right.

But he wasn't. His tie was too tight and he was starting to get annoyed with his brother's continued absence, but he was far from anxious.

He'd been wanting to marry Misty for too long— longer than he'd even realized until recently—to think about backing out now. If he had his way, he and Misty would be standing at the altar already, saying their vows. Then he would be that much closer to whisking her away on their honeymoon.

He'd wanted to take her somewhere such as Paris or Greece, but since she was already five months into her pregnancy and had suffered complications early on, it was recommended that she not fly very far.

Actually, the doctor had said it would probably be okay, but Cullen had nixed the idea. He might not be a nervous groom, but he was an exceptionally nervous and overprotective father-to-be.

They'd already flown back to Vegas once so that she could gather more of her belongings and deal with a few aspects of the dance school, but he didn't want to risk letting her board another plane until after the baby was born.

So instead, they were spending a long, uninterrupted week at the Carlyle, right in Manhattan. She'd never been there and had always wanted to see the inside of the luxury hotel.

And see the inside of it, she would. Once he got her to their suite, he didn't plan to let her leave—not even for a meal—for at least forty-eight hours.

And God help any member of his family who dared to disturb them. He had already threatened them with dire consequences if they so much as tried.

Blowing out a huff of breath, he checked his watch and went back to pacing along the edge of the circular drive that fronted the foyer entrance of the Tides.

Where the hell was Bryan?

His brother should have been there an hour ago. He had the rings for the ceremony, and they were supposed to take their places at the front of the church well before Misty walked down the aisle.

He was about to go back inside to try reaching Bryan on the phone when he heard tires squeal and an engine rev. Next thing he knew, Bryan's silver Jaguar Xje careened up the drive and skidded to a stop sideways behind another car parked several feet away.

Cullen rolled his eyes at his brother's dramatic entrance and started forward with purpose.

"It's about time," he said as Bryan opened the driver's side door and climbed out.

He was dressed in worn, comfortable looking jeans and a plain blue button-down shirt. He also had a split lip, and when he moved to slam the car door closed, Cullen noticed he was walking with an obvious limp.

"What happened to you?" Cullen asked, halting in his tracks.

Bryan shook his head. "Fender bender," he said casually. "I knew I was running late, and wasn't paying close enough attention on my race to get here.

Of course, having to stop and exchange insurance information didn't exactly help matters."

Cullen glanced from where Bryan was poking gently at his split lip to the bumper of his car. Not a scratch anywhere that Cullen could see, front, back or side. And the cut on his face was already scabbed over.

Cullen's brows drew together and he'd opened his mouth to question his brother further when Bryan slapped him on the back.

"Come on, little brother. It's time for me to get changed into my monkey suit, and for you to tie the knot."

Cullen's gut dipped in anticipation as they headed back to the house. The Tides was a sprawling, two-story stone structure bought by Patrick Elliott forty years before. Located on five acres on a bluff above the Atlantic Ocean, the entire house had been lovingly decorated and filled with family photographs and memorabilia by Cullen's grandmother, Maeve.

Throwing together and carrying out a ceremony of this size with only two weeks' notice had been no simple feat, but there had never been a question that it might be held anywhere other than the family estate. His mother had taken her role as wedding planner seriously, clearing every detail with him or Misty, but not letting her soon-to-be daughter-in-law raise a finger.

Cullen couldn't remember the last time he'd seen his mother so excited or determined. She was obviously thrilled at the idea of seeing her younger son married and expecting a child in only four more months.

And Patrick had, surprisingly, been more than willing to allow the event to be held on his property. At the very least, he hadn't put up a fuss.

Ever since he and Misty had announced their engagement, Cullen had expected a call or visit from his grandfather. A lecture about the evils of mixing his fine Elliott blood with that of a lowly showgirl. A demand that he call things off and send Misty and the baby off to be hidden away from the rest of the world, someplace where they wouldn't bring embarrassment to the family.

He'd been braced for it, ready to defend his future wife to his last breath, if necessary. But Patrick hadn't called, and he hadn't stopped by Cullen's office at EPH to confront him.

Cullen hoped his grandfather's silence meant he had accepted Misty's addition to the Elliott family, but a part of him was still waiting for the inevitable.

He and Bryan made their way across the marble foyer to the library and master suite behind it. The groomsmen were using it as their changing area, while Misty and her bridesmaids occupied one of the upstairs bedrooms. Amanda had insisted on the wide separation to avoid any chance of the groom accidentally seeing the bride in her gown before the ceremony.

The old wives' tale about bad luck befalling them if such a thing happened didn't worry Cullen. He didn't believe anything could ruin their day, or the many glorious years they had ahead of them.

The wedding itself was being held outside, on the pristine back lawn. A dark pink satin aisle had been laid on the grass, with chairs set up on either side, draped in a lighter pink fabric. A trellis stood at the end with red roses climbing over the white latticework.

"Hurry up," he told his brother, shoving a garment bag with the last remaining tux at his chest. "You've held me up long enough, and I don't want Misty thinking I got cold feet."

"Are you kidding me?" Bryan retorted. "You chased her so hard, I'm surprised you didn't just elope on your last trip to Vegas."

"It crossed my mind, believe me," Cullen muttered. It would have saved everyone a hell of a lot of trouble, and if they'd done that, Misty would have his ring on her finger and be Mrs. Cullen Elliott right now.

They would be at home, snuggled in bed or holding hands over their breakfast plates, discussing names for their future little bundle of joy. And he wouldn't be chomping at the bit to get out there and say *I do* already.

Bryan unbuttoned his shirt and kicked off his boots. "You'd have to be barefoot in Antarctica to get cold feet, and Misty knows it. You two are so damn happy together, everyone around you needs a shot of insulin to keep from going into sugar shock. It's sickening."

A small smile stole across his face. "Yeah," he agreed softly. "I know."

Cullen slapped the black tuxedo pants into his brother's hands as soon as Bryan kicked out of his jeans. "Now shut up and get dressed."

Misty stared at her reflection in the full-length mirror and felt her heart stop.

She couldn't believe this was her wedding day. That in less than half an hour, she would be walking through this massive house that intimidated her right down to her fishnet stockings, and across the expertly manicured lawn toward Cullen.

Her future husband. The man of her dreams.

In all the years she'd been with him, been secretly in love with him, she had never truly believed they could ever be together. But now she knew they would never be apart.

Despite their differences—age, upbringing, social status—she knew that he loved her. And there was no doubt that she loved him.

He'd been willing to give up his family for her— or his grandfather, at least—and his life in New York so they could be together. Compared to that, giving up her dance studio in Henderson and moving to Manhattan to try her hand at being an Elliott wife seemed a small price to pay.

And she knew she could be happy here. His entire family might not be thrilled that they were getting married, but most of them accepted her and had already made it clear they supported Cullen's decision.

She had no intention of being a housewife or

stay-at-home mother, though. She was content to stick close to the Upper West Side town house until the baby was born—and maybe for a time after. But she and Cullen had also discussed the possibility of her getting a job as a dance instructor somewhere, or perhaps opening another studio of her own in the city.

She wasn't sure yet what she wanted to do. She only knew that she didn't want her options limited just because she'd agreed to marry into the Elliott clan.

"You look beautiful." Breaking into Misty's thoughts, Bridget came up behind her and slipped into the mirror's limited view.

Her heart began to race again and she swallowed past the lump in her throat. "Are there people out there?" she asked timidly.

"Of course," Bridget offered with a laugh. "You're about to marry into the esteemed Elliott family. No one who's anyone would dare miss it. Relatives from both families are here, along with any member of the media who could beg, borrow or steal an invitation. Your mother hasn't stopped crying since she got here, by the way. Come Monday morning, your face and Cullen's will be plastered on the cover of every newspaper and magazine in America."

"Oh, God." Misty fought the urge to bend over and stick her head between her knees—mostly because, these days, bending wasn't as easy as it used to be.

"Relax." Bridget patted her back and fussed with the folds of Misty's white gown.

Misty had at first resisted the idea of wearing white on her wedding day. It seemed somewhat improper and not the tiniest bit ridiculous, considering she was five months pregnant and looked as if she'd swallowed a volleyball. But Cullen's mother had insisted, and Misty had finally agreed once she'd tried on the dress for the first time.

The entire gown was made of the same silky satin, but the smooth, unadorned bodice ended just below her breasts in the empire fashion and an overlay of gossamer with tiny seed pearls fell to her ankles, almost entirely masking the bulge of her belly.

"You look amazing," Bridget continued in an attempt to allay her fears. "All you need to remember is that this day is for you and Cullen, no one else. When you walk out there, pretend you're the only two people in the world. Keep your eyes on him and ignore everything else."

When she put it that way, Misty didn't think she'd have any trouble getting through the ceremony, no matter how many guests were watching or how many flashbulbs were going off in her face. To her, having eyes only for Cullen was as natural as breathing or waking up in his arms.

She gave herself a final once-over in the long oval looking glass, nodded and turned to face the woman who was quickly becoming her new best friend.

Bridget was wearing one of the strapless lilac brides-maids' gowns Amanda had chosen, her blond hair swept up and decorated with sprigs of spring flowers.

"Thank you. And thank you for all of your help this morning. I couldn't have done it without you."

Bridget had picked her up at Cullen's town house bright and early, whisking her away to the Tides for what would turn out to be several hours of bridal preparations. She'd done Misty's nails, hair and makeup, then even helped her get dressed when it became obvious Misty couldn't see her feet, let alone slip into delicate stockings or a handmade, nearly priceless gown.

The other woman grinned. "That's what maids of honor are for."

They were gathering Misty's bouquet and getting ready to head downstairs when a light knock sounded on the bedroom door. Bridget hurried over, prepared to bar the groom's entrance on the off chance Cullen had decided to risk his mother's wrath and try to get a peek at the bride before the ceremony.

"Granddad," she said flatly, stepping back to let the older man inside.

Patrick Elliott was tall, with short gray hair, and though Misty knew him to be in his late seventies, he looked about ten years younger. His eyes were a twinkling blue, making it clear who had passed that color on to most of the other Elliotts.

She'd only met him once before, at a small Elliott family gathering where Cullen had stayed by her side and remained staunchly protective of her. And though Parick had been cool toward her that day, he hadn't seemed outwardly hostile.

Today he was dressed in a crisp gray suit and looked only slightly nervous about entering a room that was so clearly the domain of wedding-minded women.

"I'd like a private word with the bride-to-be, if that's all right," he said.

His voice was deep, but not as gruff or demanding as one might expect from others' description of him.

Bridget crossed her arms over her chest belligerently. "I don't think—"

But Misty interrupted. "Of course."

Every anxiety that Bridget's encouraging words had managed to calm flared to life again in screaming apprehension, but she would never refuse to speak to Cullen's grandfather. Not even if she expected that she was about to get the dressing-down of a lifetime.

The man had made it clear—albeit through second parties—that he disapproved of her. Of her upbringing, her choice of career, her involvement with Cullen. But he was still going to be her relative by marriage, and he would be her child's great-grandfather by blood. The least she could do was let him speak his piece.

But no matter what he said to her, or how upsetting the encounter might turn out to be, she was still going to walk downstairs and outside and exchange vows with the man she loved.

"Are you sure?" Bridget asked, doubt, concern and more than a little loathing of her grandfather written clearly on her face.

Misty forced the corners of her mouth to curve

upward in a show of confidence she didn't entirely feel. "I'm sure."

With a reluctant nod, Bridget opened the door again. "I'll be right out here if you need me."

She cast her grandfather one last distrustful glance, then disappeared into the hallway.

Patrick watched her go, then turned back to Misty. "Thank you."

She inclined her head, her mouth too dry with uneasiness to speak.

He looked around the room, taking in all the signs of wedding day preparations. Discarded clothes and shoes, flower arrangements, trays of makeup, nail polish and perfume. Then his eyes moved back to Misty, sliding down her shapely frame, only to settle on the swollen bump at her middle.

"I've seen a change in my grandson since the two of you started seeing each other." He stuffed his hands in his pants pockets and rocked back on his heels, clearing his throat before saying more. "I started to notice it a few years ago, when he first took up with you, I believe, but it's become more obvious since you came to New York and moved in with him."

Misty's pulse was pounding so hard it echoed in her ears. She opened her mouth, closed it in hopes of creating enough saliva to form words, then opened it again.

"I'm sorry," she told him. "I know you don't approve of Cullen's involvement with me, but—"

The elderly man shook his head, his brows

coming together sharply and his mouth turning down in a frown. "That's not what I mean. What I'm trying to tell you is that Cullen seems happier these days, more at ease. He obviously loves you very much, and is excited about this baby."

He nodded in the general direction of her stomach and made an all-encompassing up and down gesture with one hand.

"You've been good for him. Even a hardheaded old man like myself can see that."

He cleared his throat again, and this time Misty realized he was nervous. Patrick Elliott, patriarch of one of the wealthiest, most influential families in New York, was uncomfortable around her.

Her, a former Las Vegas showgirl from a humble background who'd become his grandson's mistress, for heaven's sake. She found it almost beyond belief.

"I'm glad you're joining the family," he added in a harsh tone. "I have a feeling you'll do us all some good."

Stunned, Misty could only stare, wide-eyed for a moment. And then she forced herself to offer a feeble, "Thank you."

"Yes, well…" Patrick's gaze darted around the room as he began backing toward the door. "That's all I wanted to say, really. You look lovely, by the way, and I'm sure Cullen is eager to get this show on the road, so I'll leave you to…whatever it is you were doing."

He waved in her direction one last time before escaping the same way Bridget had, leaving Misty standing in stunned silence. Two seconds later, Bridget returned, casting a wary glance at her grandfather's retreating back through the crack in the door before closing it behind her.

"What did *he* want?" she asked cynically.

Misty tried to shake off the shock of Patrick's strained declaration, but seemed incapable of movement.

Cullen's grandfather hadn't apologized for the comments he'd made soon after her arrival in New York—the ones about no Elliott marrying a stripper. But he had approached her today, privately, when he didn't have to. He had welcomed her—in his own way—to the family.

"He better not have said anything to upset you," Bridget growled protectively. "If he did, I swear—"

"No." Misty shook her head, blinking several times in an attempt to clear the fog of astonishment from her brain. "You'll never believe it, but—"

Off to the side, a cell phone chirped.

"Oh, damn, that's mine."

Bridget bustled off toward the bed, digging her purse out from under the mountain of clothing that had been tossed there while the bridal party changed into their gowns.

She found her phone and flipped it open, lifting it to her ear. "Hello?"

Misty watched as Bridget riffled through her bag for a pad and pen, taking notes while she listened to whoever was on the other end of the line.

"All right. Yes. Thank you."

She closed the phone, returned it to her purse and spun back to Misty, fiddling with a few loose strands of Misty's hair, tucking them under the rhinestone headpiece where they belonged.

"You'll never believe this," she said almost breathlessly. "I just got some information about what could be a very big break on the story I'm working on for my book. It means I'll have to leave right after the reception, though."

Misty frowned in concern. "Where are you going?"

"I don't want to say just yet, but I promise to call as soon as I get there to let you know I'm all right."

She took a step back and smiled encouragingly. "Now, tell me what Granddad said so I know whether I need to sic Cullen on him or not."

Misty took a deep breath and shared what she still wasn't entirely sure had happened. "He told me I was good for Cullen and said he was glad to have me in the family."

"*What?* Are you serious?" Bridget's blue eyes were round with surprise. And then they narrowed with suspicion. "That doesn't sound like my grandfather. Are you sure you heard him correctly?"

Misty chuckled. "Yes, I'm sure. Although I admit I was as shocked as you are."

For a second, Bridget continued to scowl. Then her expression brightened and she shrugged one slim bare shoulder. "Maybe he's finally coming to his senses. Whatever the reason for his change of heart,

I'm happy for you. The rest of us always knew you'd be a wonderful addition to the family. Cullen loves you, and that's all that matters."

At the mention of Cullen's name and the reminder of how much he loved her, Misty's mouth curved up in a grin. "I know."

"Should we go downstairs and tell them we're ready to get this party started?"

Her fingers flexing around the base of her rose and lily bridal bouquet with strips of pink ribbon hanging nearly to the floor, she nodded. "Yes, let's."

With her hand in Bridget's and butterflies dive-bombing low in her belly, Misty left the room, walked down the hall and stairs to the lower level of the sprawling mansion, and toward the back of the house where her other bridesmaids were waiting to precede her down the makeshift aisle.

Bridget left her at the back of the gathering, rushing around to match up each bridesmaid, including herself, with the appropriate groomsman.

Cullen's father, Daniel, would be escorting Misty down the aisle, and as he approached, she saw a glint of emotion dampening his eyes. Close to tears already, she quickly looked away, linking her arm with his and busying herself with the folds of her gown and ribbons of her bouquet.

Once everyone was lined up and ready to go, Amanda gave the signal for the orchestra to begin playing "The Wedding March." As the first strains began, Misty's heart lurched in her chest, and she had to tell herself over and over again to take deep breaths and relax.

She may not have wanted to step outside and have hundreds of guests gawk at her, but she most certainly wanted to get to the end of this day and finally be Mrs. Cullen Elliott.

The minute she saw him, standing in front of the flower-strewn trellis at the other end of the pink pathway, her nerves left her. A sense of calm swept over her entire body and a gentle smile curved her lips.

Cullen smiled back, and from that moment on, they had eyes only for each other.

When they reached the minister, Daniel kissed her cheek, then turned her over to Cullen. Their fingers twined and he gave her hand a gentle squeeze. She squeezed back, never taking her gaze from the man she was about to marry.

The minister spoke of love and commitment, and before she knew it, it was time for them to exchange their vows. In turn, they each promised to love, honor and cherish, which Misty knew would never be a problem for either of them. And then the minister told Cullen he could kiss the bride.

"My pleasure."

Cupping her face in both hands, he leaned forward until their breaths mingled. "I love you," he whispered, for her ears only.

She blinked rapidly, feeling her heart swell near to bursting inside her chest. "I love you, too."

And then he was kissing her, a soft, chaste

meeting of their mouths that still managed to convey all the passion and devotion their future together would hold.

Epilogue

"That was some pretty incredible newlywed sex," Cullen said, combing the hair away from his damp brow before pressing a line of kisses down Misty's throat, chest, the underside of her breast.

They were in their suite at the Carlyle, blessedly alone. The wedding reception had dragged on forever—at least it had seemed that way to Cullen—until at last he'd been able to whisk Misty away.

A limo had brought them back into the city, and he'd had the honor of carrying her—in all her bridal finery—into the hotel lobby, up in the elevator and across the threshold to the honeymoon suite.

She'd protested that she was too heavy, too largely pregnant, but to him she was as light as a feather.

Even if she hadn't been, the adrenaline pumping through his veins would have allowed him to carry her the entire length of Manhattan.

Not one to overlook even the smallest detail, his mother had made sure that the room was filled with fresh flowers, gourmet chocolates and two bottles of chilled champagne—one regular and one nonalcoholic.

It was lovely, and everything a newly married couple could hope for, but Cullen had barely given it a second glance.

Instead, he'd carried his new bride straight to the king-size bed and slowly peeled the pristine white gown from her luscious body, languorously making love to her for the first time as her husband. The experience had been so moving, so elemental, he'd wanted to cry.

The second time, he had realized that Misty really and truly belonged to him. Forever.

He was one hell of a lucky man.

"If I'd known," he added, "I'd have wrangled you down the aisle years ago."

She laughed, the sound skating down his spine like chips of ice while she rubbed the back of his calf with the arch of her foot.

"I still can't believe you wore fishnet stockings under your gown."

When he'd run his hand under her dress, only to find the sexy, revealing things covering her shapely thighs, it had been quite a surprise. But in a good way. A very good way.

"I thought they were appropriate," Misty said. "As a reminder that even though you made me an Elliott today, I'll still always be a showgirl at heart."

"Amen to that," he muttered with feeling.

And then his hands began to wander again. His palms circled and stroked the taut mound at her middle, followed by his lips. "Have I ever told you how sexy I find your pregnant belly?"

"I don't think so," she said with a chuckle, feathering her fingers through his hair.

"I love touching it, feeling the baby move inside and knowing I played a part in putting it there."

"You certainly did."

"And now we have the birth to look forward to. Diaper changes and midnight feedings. Maybe even siblings."

Keeping his hand on her stomach, he kissed a trail back up to her mouth. "Have you thought of any names yet?"

"No," she answered, looking drowsy and sated, lying naked on the silky sheets. "Have you?"

"A few. And I'm sure my family will have some suggestions of their own."

He was watching her sparkling emerald eyes, so he saw the slight shuttering of her gaze at the mention of his family.

"What's the matter?" he asked.

She shook her head, her teeth toying distractedly with her bottom lip.

A stab of concern hit him low in the gut. "Tell me," he said, stilling his caress of her body.

"It's nothing bad, I just didn't have a chance to tell you before the wedding."

Releasing a breath, she turned her head on the pillow, looking him straight in the eyes. Her arm moved until she found his hand and linked their fingers together.

"Your grandfather came upstairs to see me before the ceremony."

Cullen reared back, shocked to the soles of his feet. "What? What did he say to you? Did he upset you? Threaten you? Did he offer you a bribe not to marry me?"

"No. No, no," she quickly assured him, stroking her free hand over his bare shoulder in a soothing gesture. "That's the thing. He was nice to me, and sort of…welcomed me to the family. I think."

For a few seconds, all he could do was stare down at her as though he'd been smacked between the eyes with a brick.

"Well, I'll be damned," he finally found voice enough to mutter. "I have to admit, I never expected Granddad to come around. I'm glad, though."

He pushed the hair back from her brow and lightly kissed the corner of her mouth. "Now do you believe me when I say you'll make a fine Elliott?"

"I don't know. But it certainly is a relief to know your grandfather doesn't hate me anymore…and won't end up hating you in the process."

"Wouldn't matter if he did," he replied confidently. "You're mine, and I won't let anyone tell me we can't be together."

She brought her hand from the back of his head to hold out in front of them—her left hand, with its obscenely large diamond ring and bright gold wedding band flashing in the light of the bedside lamp. And then she touched that same hand to the side of his face.

"Here's to four years as your mistress," she murmured, "and the rest of my life as your wife."

"I'll drink to that," he said before covering her mouth with his own. "Later."

* * * * *

Don't miss the next book in
THE ELLIOTTS, *HEIRESS BEWARE*
by Charlene Sands,
available in June 2006 from Silhouette Desire.

This riveting new saga begins with

In the Dark

by national bestselling author

JUDITH ARNOLD

The party at Hotel Marchand is in full swing when the lights suddenly go out. What does head of security Mac Jensen do first? He's torn between two jobs—protecting the guests at the hotel and keeping the woman he loves safe.

A woman to protect. A hotel to secure. And no idea who's determined to harm them.

On Sale June 2006

Page-turning drama…

Exotic, glamorous locations…

Intense emotion and passionate seduction…

Sheikhs, princes and billionaire tycoons…

This summer, may we suggest:

THE SHEIKH'S DISOBEDIENT BRIDE
by Jane Porter

On sale June.

AT THE GREEK TYCOON'S BIDDING
by Cathy Williams

On sale July.

THE ITALIAN MILLIONAIRE'S VIRGIN WIFE

On sale August.

With new titles to choose from every month,
discover a world of romance in our books written
by internationally bestselling authors.

Paying the Playboy's Price

(Silhouette Desire #1732)

by

EMILIE ROSE

Juliana Alden is determined to have her last—
her only—fling before settling down. And she's
found the perfect candidate: bachelor Rex Tanner.
He's pure playboy charm…but can she afford
his price?

Trust Fund Affairs: They've just spent a fortune—
the bachelors had better be worth it.

Don't miss the other titles in this series:

EXPOSING THE EXECUTIVE'S SECRETS (July)
BENDING TO THE BACHELOR'S WILL (August)

On sale this June from Silhouette Desire.

*Available wherever books are sold, including most
bookstores, supermarkets, discount stores and drugstores.*

COMING NEXT MONTH

#1729 HEIRESS BEWARE—Charlene Sands
The Elliotts
She was about to expose her family's darkest secrets, but then she lost her memory and found herself in a stranger's arms.

#1730 SATISFYING LONERGAN'S HONOR—
Maureen Child
Summer of Secrets
Their passion had been denied for far too many years. But will secrets of a long-ago summer come between them once more?

#1731 THE SOON-TO-BE-DISINHERITED WIFE—
Jennifer Greene
Secret Lives of Society Wives
He didn't know if their romantic entanglement was real, or a ruse in order to secure her multimillion-dollar inheritance.

#1732 PAYING THE PLAYBOY'S PRICE—Emilie Rose
Trust Fund Affairs
Desperate to break free of her good-girl image, this society sweetheart bought herself a bachelor at an auction. But what would her stunt really cost her?

#1733 FORCED TO THE ALTAR—Susan Crosby
Rich and Reclusive
Her only refuge was his dark and secretive home. His only salvation was her acceptance of his proposal.

#1734 A CONVENIENT PROPOSITION—Cindy Gerard
Pregnant and alone, she entered into a marriage of convenience… never imagining her attraction to her new husband would prove so *in*convenient.

SDCNM0506